For Dead Men Only

Paula Paul

All rights reserved. No part of this publication may be reproduced or transmitted in any form or by any means, electronic or mechanical, including photocopy, recording, or any information storage and retrieval system, without the prior written permission of the publisher, except in the case of brief quotations for reviews. No part of this book may be scanned, uploaded, or distributed via the Internet, without the publisher's permission and is a violation of International Copyright Law and subjects the violator to severe fines and/or imprisonment.

FOR DEAD MEN ONLY
Copyright 2019 by Paula Paul
ISBN
9781798421895

This book is a work of fiction. The names, characters, places, and incidents are products of the writer's imagination or have been used fictitiously and are not to be construed as real. Any resemblance to persons living or dead, actual events, or locale is entirely coincidental.

Published in the United States of America

Griffith Publishing
1405 Temile Hill Pl NE
Albuquerque, NM 87112

FOR DEAD MEN ONLY

By Paula Paul

Prologue

Soon Jeremy Fitzsimmons would return to the temple, but first, he wanted to devour her with all of his senses. He had spotted her through the mist as he was walking from his seaside house. She was a lovely specter, so fair, so delicate she seemed to have been spun from silk Her dark hair loosened from its pins and fell down her back as she turned to face the sea, holding her bonnet in her hand. The breeze lifted the dark mane slightly and floated strands across her face. He knew that face well, knew the patrician lines of it, the emeralds that were her eyes, the blush of her cheeks against creamy white skin. He had often admired the curve of her breasts above her bodice, her delicate hands, the cruel sound of her laughter.

Behind her, in the distance was the temple, a dark swelling of hard stone with the Cyclops eye of God staring in judgment from between the two pillars of Boaz and Jachin. He should leave now and return there, but he knew she hadn't seen him, and as long as she was distracted, he could watch her unnoticed. He could fully take in the way she moved, her limbs gliding beneath billowing skirts while her hips undulated. He could secretly study the ivory tower that was her neck, the nip of her waist.

He continued to watch as she turned her back to the sea, and it struck him that everything about her was turned away from all openness. He had wanted her to open her heart to him.

There were times when he'd even imagined she loved him, but in the next moment she might slash his soul with a scornful glare. He was fainthearted, she said, weak, cowardly.

He saw that her eyes were fixed on the temple, or more precisely, one of the four rounded protrusions at each corner that housed the secret chambers. The intensity of her gaze made him uneasy, as if her jade stare could somehow defile the secret chambers. Of course the temple was no place for women.

The wind tore her bonnet from her hand and pulled more strands of her hair around to caress her face. Even as she walked away, moving parallel to the sea, she never turned back to fetch her bonnet. When she was almost out of sight, he turned from his original route and plucked the bonnet from the bramble that had grabbed it, holding it close to his chest for a moment before he resumed his route and walked away from her and toward the Temple of the Ninth Daughter.

The dark stone building rose to a height of four stories and sat on a low hill covered with brush and trees at the edge of the village of Newton-Upon-Sea. Its distance from the main part of the village, and its imposing height gave it an air of aloofness and mystery. There were thirteen lichen-covered stone steps situated between the pillars Boaz and Jachin, the same names given to the pillars of the ancient Temple of Solomon.

Using his key, Fitzsimmons unlocked the heavy wooden doors and pushed both of them open. He felt a rush of cold air and took in the familiar heavy scent of things ancient and mystical. It took a moment for his eyes to adjust to the darkness, and he could make out the altar in the middle, a velvet rope defining its boundaries. Behind it, a distance away was the ornately carved throne of the Grand Master. His throne. Two curved stairways leading up to the secret chambers flanked the throne. A double row of chairs lined the side walls that seemed to hover

over the hall. The walls were etched in red, gold, and black figures, some of them oddly Egyptian, along with a depiction of the Paschal Lamb, a knight astride a horse, the Rose Croix, and the sacred blue slipper.

Above the throne was a large carving of the square and compasses surrounding the letter G that stood for both the one God and for the holy and sacred discipline of geometry.

The sound of Fitzsimmons' footsteps on the stone floor echoed from the dark and ornate walls as he walked across the long space to the altar where he placed the bonnet. He was startled when he noticed someone watching him—a figure slouched in the corner. He immediately retrieved the bonnet, fearing the person watching him would think he had defiled the altar. Naturally, the watcher would be a fellow Freemason. There would be no reason for anyone else to enter the temple. Fitzsimmons, as Grand Master of the Masonic Lodge of the Ninth Daughter in Newton-upon-Sea, knew that better than anyone.

"Who's there?" he shouted, and in the same moment recognized the figure as Saul Mayhew. "Brother Mayhew, why are you—"

Mayhew slowly slipped to the floor, and Fitzsimmons, when he saw the gaping mouth and unblinking eyes, realized he was dead. Saul wore his Masonic apron. Fitzsimmons gasped when he saw that the apron that symbolized purity and cleanliness had been defiled with dried blood, yet there was no sign of a wound on Saul's body.

Chapter 1

The official cause of the death of Saul Mayhew was heart attack. Since she was not called to examine the body, it never occurred to Dr. Alexandra Gladstone, to question Constable Robert Snow's conclusion. The constable had mentioned a bit of dried blood on the man's Masonic apron but said it had no bearing on his death, since it was obviously an old stain.

Nancy, her nurse and maid-of-all-work, commented on the announcement. "Never knew Mr. Mayhew had heart problems. Rather young for that, actually. Not much passed thirty," she mused as she and Alexandra sat in the parlor, sipping tea at the end of a busy day of seeing patients.

They both welcomed the temporary respite from their duties and household chores. Today they'd seen three cases of barber's itch, and Alexandra had prescribed an oxalic acid wash in each case, along with her repeated caution not to share towels at the barber's shop and to make certain the men provide their own razors, since the disease was highly contagious. Anna Speigle, a young mother, had brought her six-year-old son, convinced he was infected with small pox. It was Nancy, in this case, who had pointed out that the pustules lacked the middle indentation characteristic of small pox and was instead most likely chicken pox. Anna left, much relieved, with instructions to give her son baking soda baths. There were also the usual complaints of gout and rheumatism and numerous scrapes and bruises which the two of them dealt with routinely.

The relationship between Alexandra and Nancy did not quite follow the orthodox regimen of mistress and maid. They'd been friends since childhood and often dropped some of the customary formality.

"Mr. Mayhew seldom came to the surgery with any complaint," Alexandra said in response to Nancy's observation, "but heart disease can be a silent killer and no respecter of age." Alexandra picked up a paper from the table next to her to read while Nancy settled in with a romantic novel. It was their custom to relax just so in the parlor before bedtime.

Dr. Alexandra Gladstone was the only doctor in the village of Newton-upon-Sea in Essex. She'd taken over the medical practice of her late father. Although she had an equal amount of training and experience, perhaps even more, she was not allowed to use the title of Physician. She was forbidden for no other reason than that she was female. That was astonishing to some people, given that the nineteenth century had progressed beyond eight decades. It was not particularly astonishing to most of the citizens of Newton-upon-Sea, however. They were, in general, quite content to have things done the old way. It was difficult enough for them to adjust to the idea of the first Dr. Gladstone dying and even more difficult, for some, that he'd left his practice in the hands of this daughter. It had never occurred to any of them that a woman could be a doctor. Now, even though almost five years had passed since her father's death, Alexandra was still struggling to earn the trust of some of the citizens.

The paper she was reading explored the possibility of the existence of several pathogens that could not be seen with a microscope, referred to as viruses. She might not have given Saul Mayhew another thought all night, had not Jeremy Fitzsimmons knocked on her front door.

Zack, Alexandra's Newfoundland, stood up to his full enormous height and barked once. Two barks would have meant a patient was knocking at the surgery door near the back of the house.

Nancy placed a hand on the dog's massive head to reassure him and went to open the door.

"Good evening, Mr. Fitzsimmons," she said when she saw him standing outside the entrance.

"I must see Dr. Gladstone." Fitzsimmons moved himself into the doorway without being invited. "This is not a medical call but a personal one." He was stretching his neck, doing his best to see around Nancy, who was doing her best to block him.

"Dr. Gladstone is resting at the moment," Nancy said, sounding both polite and protective.

"I have an urgent matter I must discuss with the doctor," he insisted. "A most urgent personal matter."

Nancy was about to protest again when Alexandra entered the vestibule behind her. "How can I help you?" Alexandra asked as Nancy reluctantly stepped aside.

"I'm Jeremy Fitzsimmons," he said, while both hands fumbled with his fashionable bowler.

"Of course, Mr. Fitzsimmons, I remember you," Alexandra said, grateful that he'd given her a name to go with his familiar face. "You came to me once with a sprained ankle."

"Yes, yes," Mr. Fitzsimons said. "Clumsy accident, but that's not why I'm here. It's about. . . ." He paused and glanced toward Nancy, seemingly unwilling to continue.

Alexandra hastened to reassure him. "It's all right. You may speak in front of Nancy. She is my nurse."

"As I said, it's not a medical matter. It's. . . ."

"Yes, Mr. Fitzsimmons?"

"It's about Saul Mayhew," he blurted out after an uneasy pause.

Of course Alexandra had heard that Saul had been found dead in the chambers of the Freemasons' temple, and Jeremy Fitzsimmons was the Grand Master of the lodge. Naturally he would be upset.

"Please come in. Nancy will fetch some tea," Alexandra said, leading him into the parlor. "Mr. Mayhew was a friend of yours, I believe."

"He was a member of the lodge. A fellow Freemason," Fitzsimmons said, settling himself into the wingback fireside chair Alexandra had indicated for him. "I'm the one who found him," he added.

"Indeed? I hadn't heard that. It must have been a terrible shock for you. Perhaps some sedative powders would help calm you. Is that why you've come?"

"I told you this is not a medical matter. I don't need your powders. I need to talk." Having grown even more agitated, he was now sitting on the edge of the chair.

"Wise of you," Alexandra said. "It's best to avoid medications when possible. Ah, look. Here's Nancy with the tea. Now, that can be soothing and is quite harmless to your body."

"Saul Mayhew did not die of a heart attack. He was murdered."

Nancy almost dropped the tea tray, but she managed to settle it on the table with no more than a rattling of the cups.

Alexandra was just as taken aback. "Murdered?"

"He was." Fitzsimmons moved deeper into the chair and let his shoulders drop as if getting the awful word out in the open had relaxed him.

Alexandra, on the other hand, had grown tense. "And what, exactly, makes you think Mr. Mayhew's death was an unnatural one?"

"He was a healthy sort," Fitzsimmons said. "Not the kind to have a heart attack."

"I'm afraid, sir, that it's not always possible to know who is or is not the sort of person to have a heart attack. It's not unheard of for people even younger than Mr. Mayhew to—"

"Someone killed him! I'm sure of it." Fitzsimmons had lost the modicum of calmness he'd managed to acquire and was almost shouting.

"If you believe there was foul play, you should speak to the constable," Alexandra said.

"Constable Snow wouldn't listen to me, either. I thought you would. That's why I came here tonight. You would know the difference between murder and a natural death. I thought you would be able to convince the constable, and then he would actually start a real investigation. But you're just like him. Won't listen. No one will listen."

"Mr. Fitzsimmons, calm yourself, please," Alexandra said. "I'm quite willing to listen." She hoped her quiet voice would soothe her guest.

It worked, at least enough for Fitzsimmons to drop his voice by a little. "You didn't examine his body, I know, and the constable said there were no marks on his body. But that doesn't prove anything."

"You're quite right. I didn't examine the body," Alexandra said. "I'm not always asked to do that, especially if there's no cause to believe the death wasn't natural. Apparently, Constable Snow didn't think—"

"Doesn't matter what he thought! Seth was killed. I'm certain of it. Just as I'm certain there'll be others who will die." He was shouting again, returning to his agitated state.

"What exactly is your reason for being so certain?" Alexandra's voice had become firmer, less placating. "I am asking you for a motive, Mr. Fitzsimmons. Why would anyone want to murder Saul Mayhew and anyone else you believe may now be in danger?"

Fitzsimmons wilted in the chair. "That I cannot tell you."

"Because you don't know?"

"Because it is impossible for me to. . .to say. It's a matter of honor, you see. I can't possibly explain to anyone who is not a. . . ." His voice trailed off to silence.

"I think it best you explain all of this to the constable," Alexandra said. "If you believe someone has a motive, then it is surely your duty to divulge whatever it is you know."

Mr. Fitzsimmons jumped to his feet. "You sound just like him. The constable kept dismissing everything I said, even though he's a fellow Freemason. Yet I am duty bound to. . . ." Fitzsimmons turned quickly and hurled himself toward the door. "I should have known. When even Robert Snow, himself a member of the brotherhood, refuses to understand, then no one will."

He left, slamming the door and rushing into the night, leaving traces of rage lingering behind him like the scent of sulfur.

The next morning Alexandra, riding her mare, Lucy, was on her way to make her first house call at the home of Riddell Crome near the edge of the village. As she neared the Masonic Temple, she heard a shriek and saw a man fleeing the building. He stumbled down the steps, falling as he ran and landing in a crumpled heap at the bottom. Alexandra urged Lucy into a run toward the fallen figure, but he was already up and standing by the time she reached him. She recognized Uriah Parr, who served as janitor for the temple. He had stopped his screeching, but his face was bloodless.

"Mr. Parr! Are you all right?" she asked, sliding from her sidesaddle as quickly as her skirts would allow.

He didn't answer but looked at her with frightened eyes. "Dead," he said finally.

"I beg your pardon."

"Master Fitzsimmons," he said. "Dead. In there. In the corner where Mayhew was."

Since Uriah seemed to be in reasonably good shape after his fall, except for a lump on his forehead, Alexandra turned away, hurrying up the stone steps to the still open doors of the temple. She stopped as she entered the massive dark hall, trying to orient herself. She'd never been inside the temple before and, in fact, had no idea of whether or not women were allowed inside. She took no time to ponder the question and quickly spotted Fitzsimmons's slumped body in a darkened corner near a curving stairway. Hurrying to his side, she saw Fitzsimmons. There were no marks on his body. Oddly, however, there was a smear of blood on the white Masonic apron he wore.

Chapter 2

"I should think an autopsy would be in order," Alexandra said to Constable Robert Snow, when he asked her to provide a thorough examination Mr. Fitzsimmons's body at the mortuary. She had arranged to have the body transferred to the funeral parlor and had sent Uriah to alert the constable.

They were standing in the large open area of the mortuary where bodies were taken for Percy Gibbs, the mortician, to prepare them for burial. Percy now waited near the table where Fitzsimmons' body lay. Alexandra always felt as if she were encased in a block of ice when she was in this room and silently chided herself for not having brought a heavier shawl. The scent of formaldehyde permeated the chamber. By now, she had gone beyond smelling the embalming chemicals and thought she could taste it.

Pulling back the sheet that covered Fitzsimmons's body, Alexandra stared at the face of the man she'd spoken with in her parlor only hours earlier. It was now the color of bismuth, and his eyes, that had sparked with anger and frustration, were now hidden behind lids taking on the look of beryl. She knew his limbs would be purple and blotched where the blood had begun to pool. It was never easy to look directly at death.

"An autopsy? At this point I'm asking you to examine the body, not perform a postmortem," Constable Snow said in his usual stern manner. He had been a school master before he became constable in Newton-upon-Sea, and he had never shed his austere demeanor. Alexandra, being female, had not been allowed to attend his school, but her father had hired him as a private tutor for her and, much to Snow's consternation, had insisted that Nancy be allowed to sit in on the lessons.

"You do at least consider it odd, do you not, that both bodies were found in the Freemasons' lodge?" she asked.

"The lodge is the body, the brotherhood. The temple is the building," the constable said, "and yes, of course, I find it odd. Troubling even. That's why I asked you to examine the body in this case."

"And I did mention, did I not, that Mr. Fitzsimmons had come to my house and was quite agitated and predicting another death?"

"You did," Snow said.

"I shall be able to perform the postmortem immediately if you give the word."

"It's out of the question for you to conduct an autopsy, as I'm sure you know," Snow said. "I shall send a telegram and ask Dr. Abercrombie to come down from Foulness on the next train."

Alexandra was not in the least surprised at the constable's response. He had steadfastly refused to allow her to perform autopsies since the day she took over her late father's medical practice. It mattered not at all to Constable Snow or to a number of others in the kingdom that she was well-trained and fully capable of the task. Once again, the fact that she was female stood in her way. It would be considered most improper for her to have such intimate contact with a male body, for all of the victims clothing would be removed.

"As you wish," she said. There was nothing to be gained by admitting to the constable that she had managed to conduct at least one such examination without his knowledge. Nothing to be gained that is, except a possibly stint in gaol.

Snow glanced at Fitzsimmons's corpse as it lay on a table in the local mortuary. "Your conclusion regarding the body?"

"The man is dead," Alexandra said.

"Impertinence doesn't become you," Snow scolded.

She heard a snort coming from Percy, who was still standing nearby. It could have meant he found her remark funny or that he agreed with the constable that she was being impertinent. Or perhaps he was suppressing a sneeze.

"Impertinent? Not at all," she said. "I have told you that I agree with you that there are no visible marks on the body. Without removing the clothing, I can't be absolutely certain, of course, and without an autopsy, my knowledge is further limited. The only conclusion I can make with certainty is that Jeremy Fitzsimmons is dead."

"Thank you, Dr. Gladstone. Nothing more is required of you." Snow spoke in his stiffest and most formal voice.

Alexandra took a second or two to comprehend that she was being dismissed before she gave the constable a slight nod of her head and turned to walk away. On her way out she noticed something crumpled on the floor. When she picked it up, she realized that it was a handkerchief with the letter *F* elaborately embroidered on the corner. It had to be Mr. Fitzsimmons' handkerchief, and it could have fallen from his pocket as his body was carried into the mortuary. She was about to turn around to take the handkerchief to Constable Snow to be placed with the dead man's other belongings when she noticed a sour odor coming from it. With a quick glance over her shoulder, she stuffed it in her medical bag and headed toward the door that led to the mortuary's outer room.

As she left the room, she heard Percy quoting scripture and sounding as if he, too, was scolding her. "The body is for the Lord and the Lord for the body." In spite of declaring he was an atheist, he had an astounding repertoire of scripture that he could quote for virtually any occasion.

She walked past the garishly painted depiction of Lazarus being raised from the dead and out the front door to where Zack waited for her, lounging on the front step. The giant Newfoundland seemed to sense her dismay and stood to nuzzle against her.

When she arrived home, the surgery's waiting room was already full of impatient patients. She and Nancy hardly had time to speak as they attended to the needs of those wanting tonics for rheumatism or herbs for a cough, a farmer with a dislocated shoulder, as well as other villagers with various complaints. It was midafternoon before the tide of ailments subsided.

"We haven't even had time to eat," Nancy said when the surgery was finally empty of patients. "No time to prepare a proper meal, either, but there's old mutton and potatoes. I'll set the table in the dining room."

"Never mind that," Alexandra said. "We'll eat in the kitchen. Call the boys in to eat with us as well," she said. She meant Artie and Rob, the two youngsters who worked in the stable taking care of her mare, Lucy, that she rode to visit patients in their homes. They had a small kitchen of their own in their rooms above the stable, but Alexandra occasionally liked to have them eat in the house. The boys also had the responsibility of keeping the house and out buildings in good repair and keeping them stocked with firewood. Before Nancy hired them, they'd both been homeless orphans who supported themselves picking pockets and stealing from fisherman at the wharves.

The two entered punching each other and giggling with each blow. Nancy quickly put a stop to it. "No way to conduct yourselves when you've been invited to dine with a lady," she scolded.

Rob, the older of the two, who claimed to be sixteen years old, snatched a cap from his head. "Sorry, Nance. Meant no disrespect to the doc." He stole a glance at Alexandra as he spoke. Artie, the eight-year-old lowered his gaze and took a step backward.

With a hand on a shoulder of each of the boys, Alexandra urged them toward the rough-hewn kitchen table. "Nancy's correct," she said. "The house is no place for playful scuffling, so let's put it aside for now and enjoy our meal."

Nancy wasn't yet ready to give up on her scolding. "Sometimes I think the two of you don't have enough to keep you busy and out of mischief." She set a platter of mutton and potatoes on the table and wiped her hands on a dish towel before she too sat down.

"Oh no, Nance," Rob protested. "We've plenty to do. A tussle now and then don't mean nuffin," he added in his thick Essex accent.

Alexandra wanted to protest that they were just being boys, but dared not undermine Nancy's instructions in front of them.

Nancy still would not let it go. "I suppose you spent the day in town or dillydallying with your old chums at the wharves," she said.

"We done no dillydallying," Artie said, speaking up for the first time. "Don't never do that."

Rob turned to him and snorted a laugh. "Don't even know what it means, does ye?"

Artie didn't answer. He was already chewing on a morsel of the mutton Nancy had just placed on his plate.

"Suppose you heard no talk of the murders then," Nancy said. Alexandra smiled to herself, knowing that Nancy was probing, trying to pick up the latest gossip since she'd been too busy during the day to question any of the patients.

"Neither of the milk cows knows much about it," Rob said. "Nanny goat knows less."

Alexandra spoke up, hoping to head of another scolding of the boys from Nancy for talking fresh. "I didn't mention, did I, Nancy, that Constable Snow sent a telegram to Dr. Abercrombie in Foulness to perform the autopsy?"

Nancy responded with a "Hmpf!" and shook her head. "Can't say I'm surprised. I'm sure he lectured you again about how 'tis not fitting for a lady to perform an autopsy."

"Did you say Abercrombie from Foulness?" Rob said before Alexandra could respond.

"Yes," Alexandra said. "Do you know him?"

"Heard of 'im," Rob said.

"They say he's a duck," Artie added.

"Don't speak with your mouthful," Nancy said.

"He means quack," Rob said. "Word is old Abercrombie is a quack of a doctor."

"How so?" Nancy asked, suddenly losing interest in Artie's chewing.

"Word is 'e cut into a woman to cure her of a belly ache and took out the wrong thing," Rob said.

"She pegged out," Artie added.

Rob nodded. "That's right. Turned up her toes, they say."

"Who said such a thing?" Alexandra asked.

Rob shrugged. "Them that knowed 'er, I reckon."

"Took out the wrong thing?" Nancy asked. "What exactly did he take out?"

"How's the likes o' me to know a thing like that?" Rob said. "I ain't no doctor."

Alexandra was about to admonish everyone at the table that the conversation was not the sort to be shared at a meal when Nancy spoke up for her. "There'll be no more of this talk for now," she said. "Take smaller bites, Artie. Elbows off the table, Rob."

It wasn't until later when they boys had retired to their quarters above the stable and Alexandra was relaxed with a book in the parlor that Nancy brought up the subject again.

"Never heard the awful tale about the doctor in Foulness," Nancy said as she placed a cup of tea on the table next to Alexandra's chair. "Had you, miss?"

"No, certainly not," Alexandra said, trying to concentrate on her book.

"'Twould be interesting, wouldn't it, to know exactly what mistake he made during surgery on that poor woman?"

"Oh, Nancy, it's probably all just idle gossip. Chances are he made no mistake at all. You know how people go on."

"In my experience, where there's smoke, there's fire," Nancy said as she sat in her customary chair opposite Alexandra. "Is it true the two men were murdered?" she asked, changing the subject as if she were fishing for something Alexandra was willing to discuss.

"That hasn't been determined yet," Alexandra said, "but the suspicion is there, as I'm sure you know."

"Of course. Everyone knows that. But what why kill those two men?"

Alexandra shook her head. "At the present, I believe any motive is unknown."

"Knowing you, Miss Alex, I'd wager you have a theory." Nancy used the address for Alexandra she'd used since they were children.

"I wish I did, Nancy, but in this case, I don't have one."

"And the cause of death?" Nancy probed.

Again, Alexandra shook her head. " I'm afraid I. . . ." She stopped in midsentence, only then remembering the odoerous handkerchief she'd retrieved from the ground in front of the mortuary.

Nancy's eyes widened. "You do know something! What is it?"

"I'm not sure," Alexandra said, "but I'd like you to have a look at what I found." She stood and walked toward the surgery, where she'd left her medical bag. Pulling the smelly handkerchief from where she'd stuffed it inside, she brought it back to Nancy.

Nancy took the cloth and examined it. "Nothing more than a hankie."

"Have a sniff."

Nancy complied but removed it quickly from her nose. "*Whew*! I'd say the man who owns this used it to wipe vomit from his mouth. Wait a bit! That's a sweet smell, too. Would you say 'tis sugar?"

"I'm not sure."

"Any idea who may have dropped it?"

"There's an *F* embroidered in the corner. See it there?"

"Fitzsimmons? Where did you find it?"

"On the floor in the mortuary after Mr. Fitzsimmons's body had been brought there from the constable's office. I suspect it fell from his pocket."

"Some poisons have a sweet smell," Nancy said.

"You've jumped to the most obvious conclusion, Nancy, and I confess that's the first thing I thought of, but of course that's no more than speculation."

"Have you told Constable Snow yet?"

"No, but I shall. Tomorrow."

"Of course." Something in Nancy's tone made Alexandra think she doubted her intention.

Rob and Artie had Lucy saddled and ready to go by the time Alexandra had finished her breakfast the next morning. The boys helped her mount as she started out on her rounds. She'd seen two of her homebound patients and had one more to visit when she remembered that Nancy had reminded her to stop by the apothecary shop for oil of turpentine to be used in poultices on the chest. Spring was just around the corner, and young William Morgan's asthma always worsened in the spring.

Giles Higginbotham, the apothecary, greeted her as she entered. "Good morning, Dr. Gladstone." Before she could even return his greeting, he continued with, "Terrible news we've had here in Newton-upon-Sea recently. Two mysterious deaths. Murder, they say."

"That hasn't been confirmed, as far as I know." Alexandra glanced around her to see if there were any others in the shop who might be drawn into the conversation. Although it could be no more than gossip, there was always the possibility of learning something important. There was only one other customer, a young woman, who seemed preoccupied with something she'd pulled from a shelf at the opposite end of the shop. Her back was turned, and Alexandra couldn't identify her.

"Plain as day," Higginbotham said. "Two of the Freemasons brotherhood. Odd, isn't it? Makes me wonder who will be next."

"I shouldn't worry about that, Mr. Higginbotham."

"Easy for you to say, since there's no possible way you could be a member of the brotherhood. Even your own father, good man that he was, was never inducted, if my memory serves me."

"Your memory serves you correctly," Alexandra said. Her father had always been too busy with his practice to contemplate membership, and he'd always professed to be against secret societies on principal.

"Then I'd say it's most likely you've nothing to worry about."

Alexandra was ready to change the subject. "Do have yellow turpentine as well as the white?" she asked. "I'll have a use for both."

"I'm a Freemason myself, so I know of what I speak," Higginbotham said, ignoring her request, "and it's no coincidence those two unfortunate souls were found dead in the temple."

"Do you also have any speculation as to why they were each found just there?" Alexandra asked, her interest again piqued.

"More than speculation, I'd say. There're reasons that harken back to ancient times, but I'm not at liberty to talk about it."

"Secrets of the brotherhood, of course."

Higginbotham said nothing as he stared straight ahead. She took that to mean he was sticking to what she disdainfully considered a secret oath. She'd inherited her father's disregard for secret societies.

"About that turpentine. . . ."

"I have both." Before Higgenbotham turned to the shelves behind him, he called out to his other customer. "I'll be with you in a moment, Miss Payne."

Alexandra saw then that he was speaking to Judith Payne, a woman who lived alone in a pretty little cottage on the opposite side of the village from Alexandra's house. Judith was probably around twenty-five years of age and unmarried, considered by many as past her prime, as was Alexandra, who was a few years older. Nevertheless, Judith was quite pretty with lively blue eyes and shining dark hair that persisted in slipping the confines of her bonnet to caress her well-shaped face. Now, however, her usually pretty face looked colorless and stricken, and she paid no heed to Higginbotham's call to her. Instead, she brushed past Alexandra and hurried from the shop.

Alexandra thought no more of it, however, as she made her purchase and walked to the street where Zack was waiting next to a tethered Lucy. She was about to mount the little mare when Judith Payne suddenly appeared from the narrow area between the apothecary shop and the harness maker next door. The poor woman looked even paler and more agonized.

"Dr. Gladstone!" she called in a trembling voice. "May I have a word with you?"

"Certainly," Alexandra said, assuming the woman was suffering from some troubling illness.

Judith moved closer and looked all around as if to make sure no one was within hearing distance. "It's about the murders," she whispered. "I know who killed them."

Chapter 3

Alexandra didn't respond at first. She was far too surprised at what she had just heard. Judith Payne's troubled expression increased her concern.

"Please explain yourself, Miss Payne."

Judith moved closer and whispered. "We can't talk here, but I must tell you something important."

"Of course," Alexandra said. "Can you be at my house at half past the hour? It's the last house on Barrow Hill Road, near the—"

"I know where your house and surgery are, Dr. Gladstone, but we cannot meet there," Judith said, interrupting. "Too much coming and going of people in and out of the surgery. I must speak to you in private."

"Where do you suggest we meet?" Alexandra asked, her curiosity growing by the second.

"My house at half past the hour? It's much closer. Number three Dedham Row, behind the church.

"Of course," Alexandra said. She watched Judith hurry away, disappearing around the corner of the building that housed the apothecary shop. Alexandra turned in the opposite direction. If she was to be at Judith Payne's house at half past one, she still had time to see her last patient if she didn't tarry now.

She rode Lucy to Olive Fontaine's house, only a short distance from the apothecary. Mrs. Fontaine was an elderly widow who lived alone with her many cats. Because she was given to mild bronchitis and frequent bouts of rheumatism, Alexandra made it a practice to visit her often.

As they approached, Zack made a low muttering growl.

"It's all right Zack," Alexandra said. "The cats won't bother you if you leave them alone."

Zack responded with another growl.

After she'd tied Lucy to a post, Alexandra, followed by a still edgy Zack, made her way up the walk through a lush, flowering garden to the front door. The sweet scent of the blossoms, birds chirping in trees, a bright yellow bee on one of the red blooms all added to the tranquility of the scene.

When Alexandra knocked at the door, Mrs. Fontaine, tall and thin and a bit stooped, welcomed her with enthusiasm and insisted she sit while she hurried off to bring her tea. Zack, as was his custom, stayed at the front door. Instead of lying down as he did when she called at other homes, he stood alert, preparing himself for any feline that might venture outdoors.

"You're looking rather spry today, Mrs. Fontaine," Alexandra said as the elderly woman handed her a steaming cup.

"No rheumatism aches for me as long as the weather cooperates. Lovely, isn't it? Except for a nip of cold breeze in the early morning." Mrs. Fontaine moved a striped kitten from her chair and held it in her lap as she sat across from Alexandra with her own tea.

"Lovely weather, indeed," Alexandra said. Mrs. Fontaine was always eager to talk, even if it was only about the weather. She no doubt missed the company of her late husband, an oysterman, as well as the fuss and bustle of her three strapping sons who had long since married and moved away.

"Already have a good stand of flowers in my garden, I have," Mrs. Fontaine said, her gnarled hands stroking the kitten. "I've acquired a few bees to help with the pollination, and they've made a remarkable difference."

Alexandra smiled. "Your garden is lovely, as usual, and you're always busy with something."

"Oh yes." Mrs. Fontaine's smile accented lines around her eyes. An elegant face, Alexandra thought. "I'm happy if I have something to care for—my garden, my cats. God gave us life, and I believe we should nourish it in all species." A large, white Persian cat jumped into Mrs. Fontaine's chair and crawled up to rest on her shoulder while a gray tomcat of mixed breed curled at her feet.

"Well said, Mrs. Fontaine."

"Sad, isn't it, that not all agree? I'm speaking of the murders of course."

"You've heard about that?"

"Oh, I've heard, recluse that I am. Hard to keep that sort of thing secret, isn't it?"

"I suppose so," Alexandra agreed. "Even though there's no actual proof the men were murdered."

"But my dear Alexandra," Mrs. Fontaine said, reverting to her first name, "How can you doubt it? You've lived here all of your life, and you must have heard all of the stories."

"I'm not certain I know what—"

"Of course! Of course!" Mrs. Fontaine said, interrupting her. "I forgot for a moment that Huntington was never a member of the brotherhood. Perhaps you wouldn't have heard." Huntington was Alexandra's father, the late Dr. Huntington Gladstone. Mrs. Fontaine was one of the few left in Newton-upon-Sea who still referred to him by his first name—indeed, one of the few who had been his contemporary.

"Excuse me, Mrs. Fontaine, what is it that I wouldn't have heard?"

"About the horseman and the old line families, the treasure."

"Old line families," Alexandra mused. "I'm not certain, but it seems to me I've heard something about a group of families in connection with the local temple and something about a buried treasure, but I thought the treasure stories were just the stuff of legends we talked about as children. Rather like believing in ghosts in that old abandoned house near the sea, but a horseman. . . ?"

"It's a long and complicated story. Has to do with geography before there was such a thing as geography, you know, and longitude and latitude lines used by the ancients. Had some mystical context. Then those lines were later used for the salt trade. Families who lived along those lines, so they say, were the families of the Templars."

"Yes, that sounds vaguely familiar, at least some of it. Could I have heard it from my father? There was something about *hal* being the Greek word for salt and place names that begin with *al* having something to do with that. Places like Alsace in France. I can't remember how it all fits together."

Mrs. Fontaine smiled slightly. "Most likely you heard that from your mother rather than your father. Your mother, I believe, was from one of the old lines."

"Perhaps," Alexandra said, "but I'm not certain. I was rather young when she died."

"Yes, I remember," Mrs. Fontaine said, giving Alexandra a sad smile.

"Now, tell me, what was it you were saying about a horseman?" Alexandra asked. Before Mrs. Fontaine could respond, an old clock on a chest behind her chimed the hour. "Oh!

Forgive me, Mrs. Fontaine, I must ask you to tell me at another time. I have an appointment. I am sure to be late if I don't leave. I've not yet asked you about your health or your needs."

Mrs. Fontaine stood as well. "My health is better than an old woman expects, and my needs are few and well met," she said as she brushed a kiss on Alexandra's cheek. "Do come back, my dear. I always look forward to your visits."

Alexandra bid her goodbye with a promise to return soon. Besides watching after her health, she now had several questions to ask that there'd not been time to get to today.

Zack stood from his perch near the front door as she exited and growled, giving one of the cats a slant-eyed stare. The cat quickly retaliated with a hiss that put Zack in his place. He backed away, only too grateful to follow along beside Alexandra as she rode Lucy toward Judith Payne's cottage on Dedham Row.

Alexandra saw a blue haze of forget-me-nots as she approached the cottage. The little garden in front, though pretty, paled in comparison to Mrs. Fontaine's garden. She noticed a jasmine and crocuses in purple and blue, and even a few green shoots of iris, but there was not the elaborate variety of Mrs. Fontaine's plantings. She tied Lucy to a post, and Zack positioned himself in a comfortable pose near the door, his chin flat to the ground, and his dark eyes still drooping a little, perhaps over embarrassment about his cowardly reaction to the cat.

After she knocked, Alexandra stood at the door for several seconds before Judith appeared. She was shown into the parlor, a room as tidy and carefully arranged as the front garden had been, but with less color. A ray of early spring sunshine splayed itself across the center of the dark-hued carpet, giving an otherwise somber chamber a welcoming look.

"Dr. Gladstone, thank you for coming," Judith said as she directed Alexandra toward a sofa. Judith's face, usually as pretty and fresh-looking as spring, today was marred with a frown and a troubled expression.

"Are you all right, Miss Payne?" Alexandra asked.

Judith pressed her lips together in a nervous gesture before she answered. "To be frank, no, I'm not all right, and please call me Judith."

"Very well, Judith. Now, please, tell me what's troubling you."

"It's those men--those who were murdered," she said, as if to remind Alexandra. Judith held her head down and twisted a white handkerchief with her long fingers and sat with the rigid posture of a schoolboy. It was several seconds more before she raised her eyes to look at Alexandra. "As I told you, I. . . .believe I know the identity of the person who killed them. She was obviously struggling to keep her voice steady, but she was not completely succeeding.

"What. . .makes you think you know that?" Alexandra asked.

"It's because of Thomas Cavenaugh," Judith blurted.

Alexandra spoke calmly, hoping to keep Judith from giving in to the tears she seemed to be on the verge of shedding. "I don't believe I know anyone by that name," she said.

"He doesn't live here in Newton, he lives in Foulness," she said, referring to the village a few miles up the coast between Newton-upon-Sea and Colchester.

"I see, and what makes you think he may have killed anyone?"

"He. . .he's my fiancé." Judith was twisting her handkerchief again. "I don't mean he's a murderer. I can't see him doing such a thing, although I don't really love him."

Alexandra frowned. "I'm afraid I don't understand at all what you're trying to tell me, Judith."

"What I'm trying to say is that my father killed those two men."

It took Alexandra a moment to respond. "Your father?" she finally managed.

Judith nodded as a tear crept down her cheek.

"Are you quite certain?"

"I am," Judith said.

"I confess, I've never met your father, but how on earth did you come to such an extraordinary conclusion?"

Judith didn't answer. "You've never met Papa because he lives in Foulness, as does Thomas Cavenaugh," she said. "I lived there as well. Before I came to Newton-upon-Sea."

Alexandra remembered Judith coming to the parish with her mother when Judith was still a young maid in her teens. Now that she was in her mid-twenties, there was much speculation as to why she never married. Alexandra could understand that Judith's life had kept her too busy for marriage. When her mother had fallen ill with consumption, Judith was no more than fifteen. She'd cared for her mother for the next several years and had taken over her mother's profession as a dress-maker to provide for both of them.

Alexandra said. "As I remember, your mother professed to be a widow."

"Yes." Judith looked at Alexandra with a forlorn expression. "It was easier for her to claim widowhood than to admit she'd left Papa."

"I see," Alexandra said.

"Women have such little control over their own lives." Judith's voice took on a note of anger. "No one could imagine how it was for her, trying to live with a man like my father. Oh no," she added quickly, "don't get the wrong impression. She loved him. We both did. I was allowed to see him from time to time, but my mother always insisted that she be present to protect me. He could be violent when he was angry."

"He hurt you?"

"Never me, but he hit my mother simply for disagreeing with him. As if she had no right to express herself. Besides that, he is an impossible man—a dreamer, unwise, incompetent. He was always full of schemes to make us rich. Even after Mama and I left, he'd show up with some unreasonable plan of some sort--a way to crossbreed cattle for more milk, a scheme to grow tea leaves in cold climates. He had all sorts of ideas about using electricity for things like growing larger plants. The money he lost on those ideas! We were barely surviving until Mother and I came here."

"I'm sorry." Alexandra said.

"You can only imagine how sorry my mother was. Especially since it was her inheritance that he squandered. Her bitterness made her ill then finally killed her."

"Judith," Alexandra said, "I can understand her bitterness, and perhaps yours as well, but being an unreasonable dreamer and schemer hardly makes a man a murderer."

Judith looked down at her hands, folded in her lap. They were well-shaped hands but a bit too brown to be the hands of a lady. They were the hands of someone who spent time outdoors. More tears fell on her slender fingers. "I wish that were true," she said and sniffed. She'd pulled a handkerchief from her sleeve and dabbed her eyes and nose. "But there was another scheme. This one a desperate one because he no longer had access to money. All of his financiers had finally given up on his crackpot ideas."

"An idea that involved murder?" Alexandra asked.

"Not at first. It involved me, though, and Thomas Cavenaugh."

"Your fiancé? Whom you don't love?"

"Of course I didn't love him. I told you, it was my father's last desperate scheme. You see, Mr. Cavenaugh is a wealthy man who once loaned my father money. Of course, Papa can't pay him, so he offered me to him. I am to be Mrs. Thomas Cavenaugh, and Papa will have a source of financing for the rest of his life."

"And you agreed to this," Alexandra said.

"Yes, I agreed, reluctantly," Judith said, dabbing at her eyes and nose again. "And before you can ask why, it was because, as I said, I love my father. When I was young, he would weave fantastic stories to entertain me, stories in which I was a beautiful princess or a great queen, or even a fairy with magical powers. He was the one who once took me to a circus, although God only knows where he got the money. I suppose you could say he bribed me into loving him. I agreed to marry Thomas when my father asked me to. I wanted to help him. I wanted him to love me as much as I love him. Surely you can understand that."

"Of course I can." Alexandra was remembering how desperately she'd wanted to please her own father. "But that still doesn't explain why you think he is a murderer."

"Both Jeremy Fitzsimmons and Saul Mayhew were courting me, you see, and I have to confess that I was pleased by their attention. But Papa couldn't afford for this attraction to go any further. He said as much. He said he'd kill anyone who ruined his chance of financial redemption. It was an opportunity for both of us, he said." Judith's voice quaked as she spoke. "You can't imagine how difficult this is for me," she added, breaking into sobs.

Alexandra went to her and took her hand. "You must try not to let it overcome you. After all, there's no proof, not even any suspects at this point. Calm yourself and let the investigation take its course."

"I. . .I can't in good conscience stay silent about this," Judith said. "I had to speak to someone, and I thought you'd understand. I admire you so much—the way you've stood up against criticism about your right to practice medicine, the fact that you refuse to admit that women are unfit for any career they might choose."

"Judith," Alexandra said with some reluctance, "I appreciate your confidence in me, but if you are convinced that what you told me about your father is true, you should tell Constable Snow."

"You're right, of course, but I can't risk anyone knowing about it if I do."

"And why is this?"

"Word could get back to my father. It could be dangerous for me."

"Surely your father wouldn't harm you. And how would it benefit him if something happened to you?"

"I used to think he wouldn't harm me, but he did strike my mother, as I told you, and now that he has resorted to murder. . . . Please," Judith said. "This is why I asked you here today. You must help me find a way to speak with the constable without anyone knowing it."

Alexandra was about to attempt to explain to her that her reasoning was flawed, but she was once again swayed by Judith's agitation. "Very well," she said. "I'll go for the constable now and send him to your house."

Judith accompanied her to the door where Zack and Lucy were waiting near the front. It was obvious Zack hadn't rested there the entire time, however. Alexandra saw chewed blossoms along the walkway.

"I'm afraid Zack has been destroying your garden," she said, embarrassed.

"Please don't concern yourself," Judith said. "Just help me."

"I'll do my best," Alexandra said. She left, riding Lucy and with Zack following along. She scolded Zack as they continued toward the constable's office in the center of the village. Zack ducked his head briefly, but he apparently thought that was sufficient apology and galumphed ahead of Alexandra and Lucy, enjoying the spring air.

She could see, as she approached the building in the oldest section of the village, that the door was closed. A sign on the door outside explained the reason.

I will be away from the office for an indefinite period attending to a matter of personal interest. A deputy has been appointed and will assume duties when possible.

The note was signed by Constable Snow.

Alexandra could hardly believe what she had read. It made no sense at all that the constable would leave town when there were two suspicious deaths to investigate.

Chapter 4

"Always was an odd bird, that Snow," said Nancy when Alexandra told her the extraordinary news. "I should think now you'd have to agree." She was busy replacing items on shelves and in drawers in the surgery, preparing for the next walk-in patient.

Alexandra looped a stethoscope around her neck. "It hardly makes sense, does it?"

"To leave the parish when there's a crazed murderer running loose? Makes sense only to him, I suppose."

Alexandra shook her head and frowned. "I can't think why he would do such a thing."

"I can think of just two possibilities." Nancy spoke with her back to Alexandra, still busy with her task at hand. "Either he's afraid he'll be next, since 'tis Freemasons the killer appears to be after, or else he's the killer himself and has nothing to fear."

Alexandra almost dropped a stack of bandages. "Nancy! How absurd. You know as well as I that, for all his oddities and foibles, Constable Snow is not a killer."

Nancy's response was a shrug.

"And as for his fearing he might be the next victim," Alexandra continued, "there are plenty of other Freemasons in Newton who could be next, if that's even the motive. However, I've just explained to you that Judith Payne offers another reason for the killings and I'm beginning to think she could be right."

Nancy turned around, wearing a look on her face that could have been interpreted as surprise at Alexandra's dense thinking. "They were both killed in the Freemasons' Lodge—the temple, as they call it. Both died in a similar manner with no marks upon their bodies. I'd say that's more than coincidence. I'd say there's a connection."

Alexandra sighed audibly. "Perhaps you're right. Or perhaps you're not right. As I told you, Judith said they were killed because they were her suitors."

Nancy shuddered. "Whatever the motive, the village is left unprotected with a mad killer on the loose."

"I'm sure Constable Snow will be back in time to take care of any further emergencies, and in the meantime, there will be a deputy in charge," Alexandra said without being as confident as she was pretending to be.

Before they could continue their discourse, a patient showed up at the surgery door. A housewife had sliced her hand on a broken tea cup and needed a few stitches. Nancy helped by suppressing the bleeding with a solution of alum and white oak bark.

Several other patients followed, and it was no surprise that the prevalent topic of conversation among them was the two deaths.

"I say 'tis the horseman what done it, killed both of 'em," Hannibal Talbot said. "Seen 'im meself, I did, on the night before young Mayhew died. Saw 'im again on the night before Fitzsimmons was kilt. He'd come in for a compound of balsam and sulfur, which Nancy concocted for him at Alexandra's direction. It was the only thing that would give him relief from the irritation of gravel in his kidneys, he claimed.

"You must reduce the amount of meat in your diet," Alexandra warned him for at least the tenth time, "and only one cup of tea a day."

"What horseman?" Nancy asked before Alexandra could finish giving her instructions to Hannibal.

"The Templar horseman," Hannibal said. "You've heard the tale, haven't you Nance? Lived here all yer life, ye have, just like me. Ask the doctor. I'm sure she's heard."

Nancy shook her head. "Can't say that I have." She glanced at Alexandra. "Have you heard anything about a Templar horseman, miss?"

Alexandra was too distracted to answer. She was making a note in Hannibal's file to add a tincture of colchicum seed if his condition didn't improve.

Hannibal scowled at both of them. "Now I find that hard to believe since the real Dr. Gladstone knew all about it. Must 'ave mentioned it to ye."

"The *real* Dr. Gladstone?" Nancy sounded incensed. "You are in the presence of the real Dr.---"

"Never mind, Nancy," Alexandra said, interrupting her. It wasn't the first time she'd heard the inference that she wasn't a *real* doctor. "Now, Hannibal, what's this about a horse?"

"Not a horse, miss, a horseman. One of the Knights Templar."

"I did hear someone mention something about a horseman, now that I think about it," Alexandra said, remembering Mrs. Fontaine's reference. "Now, Hannibal, if you're not better in two or three days, come back to see me. And don't forget about cutting back on the meat and tea."

"Knights Templar!" Nancy said, her voice full of disdain as she, along with Hannibal, appeared to dismiss Alexandra's instuctions. "They've all been gone from England for centuries."

"Well one of 'em still rides here. Or at least the ghost of one. Out by the Temple of the Ninth Daughter," Hannibal said. "You know, the Freemasons' temple. Used to be a Templar priory there. They's Templar treasure buried there, some say. That's why the horseman shows up now and then. To guard it, they says."

"Oh that old wives' tale about the treasure!" Nancy said. "I've heard that one, of course. Who hasn't? But as the first Dr. Gladstone used to say, 'tis nothing but humbug and juggery pokery."

Hannibal's face turned red with anger. "Ain't humbug and juggery pokery when men is dying for it. I knows that fer sure!"

"We can all agree that the death of two men is nothing to be taken lightly," Alexandra said in an effort to diffuse the exchange.

"Freemasons! They's all accustomed to the black arts. Don't ye know they keeps a goat in that temple? 'Tis the symbol of the devil."

"Never saw a goat around the temple," Nancy said.

"'Tis true! I heard it many times. They's plenty o' secret stuff goes on in that temple. They say they kills a man by the name o' Hiram and brings 'im back to live now and then. Dark magic, 'tis."

"Hiram Abiff," Nancy said. "Supposed to be the architect for Solomon's Temple."

"I ain't fer knowin' that. All I know is, they's secret stuff they do in that—"

"Now, Hannibal, do you understand that I want to see you again in two or three days?" Alexandra asked, hoping to end the conversation.

"I understands that all right, but if ye thinks a man's going to forego his meat and tea, then ye sure didn't learn it from the real Dr. Gladstone. Why, I'd sooner give up me pint!" He was still grumbling as he left the surgery.

"How did you know about the architect of Solomon's Temple, Nancy?" Alexandra asked after Hannibal was gone.

Nancy shrugged. "You hear all kinds of things about the Freemasons. Some of it true, some of it not, I suppose. But people are fascinated by them."

"You amaze me with what you know," Alexandra said just as Elsie Prodder showed up the surgery door. She was in no better mood than Hannibal had been and complained of a stomach ailment. "Now don't go telling me 'tis something I ate," she cautioned Alexandra. "For I know 'tis not. I have something far more dangerous eating away at me, and I wants a cure. After all, that's what you're here for, is it not?"

"I will certainly do my best, "Alexandra said. Elsie kept talking all the while Alexandra examined her, stopping only long enough to stick out her tongue when she was asked to.

"Don't know what Newton-upon-sea is coming to. First we lose our doctor, then our constable disappears right when we need 'im most. Two dead men, and he leaves! Can you fathom that? There could be more deaths with Robert Snow not here to stop it. Not that he would stop it, mind you. Couldn't stop the first two, could he? Has a streak of coward in 'im, don't he? Don't care if he did used to be a schoolmaster. Learning don't keep a man from being a coward, I always say." Elsie moved to the table where Alexandra directed her to lie down. "Take me own husband. Never learned a thing in 'is life, and neither did I, but neither of us has ever been called cowards. Stands up to anything, we does. But Robert Snow? What does he do? Runs, that's what. I say 'es scared o' dying hisself, and I don't care what Nell Stillwell says. Thinks 'e's gone off to Scotland. Ung, that hurts when you do that."

"Sorry," Alexandra said. "Tell me if it hurts again."

"Why would the constable go to Scotland?" Nancy asked. She was adjusting the sheet that had been spread over Elsie to protect her privacy.

"To visit that Orkwright woman, Nell says. Remember that one? Everyone says 'e was in love with 'er. Lived up there on that hill above the sea, she did. High falutin' woman she was. Not the kind to 'ave anything to do with the likes of old Snow. God in heaven, yes, that hurts."

Jane Orkwright had been Alexandra's friend and had moved away after her husband, Admiral George Edward Orkwright, died under unfortunate circumstances. Constable Snow had always admired Mrs. Orkwright, a gentle, refined woman, as had many people in Newton-upon-sea. Even Alexandra had wondered herself if he had been in love with her.

"Well, it wasn't Scotland 'e went off to," Elsie said. "Nell don't know of what she speaks. I happen to know 'twas London." She paused long enough for a self-satisfied chuckle followed by another groan as Alexandra prodded her stomach. "You should 'ave seen Nell's face when I told her that. Didn't like it that I found out before she did."

"London?" Nancy asked.

"The constable bought a train ticket for London. Stationmaster told me that. Ben Tottenham hisself."

"For what reason?" Nancy never hesitated to pry. Alexandra was equally as curious, but she'd never allow herself to ask.

"And how would I be knowing the answer to that?" Elsie said just as Alexandra put a stethoscope to her midsection.

"Most likely, business of the commonwealth," Nancy said.

"Commonwealth, my foot. Most likely a woman, if ye ask me."

Nancy wasn't one to let things drop. "And why would you say that?"

"Why? 'E's a man ain't 'e? Maybe ye wouldn't be knowin' about things like that, ye bein' a maiden lady, but I can tell ye, when a man—"

"It doesn't appear you have any serious problem with your stomach," Alexandra said, interrupting before the conversation further degenerated. "I believe you can find substantial relief if you forego things like butter, cream, meat fats."

Elsie was indignant. "You wants me to eat like a pauper?"

"Certainly not, but you'll feel better if you cut back on rich foods," Alexandra said.

Elsie pulled herself up to a sitting position. "What business does a doctor 'ave tellin' a body what to eat? 'Tis not yer business. 'Tis yer business to give me tonics and physics and the like."

Nancy had already pulled a bottle full of pills from the shelf. She and Alexandra had concocted them from sulfate of quinia and nux vomiea for digestive problems. She looked at Alexandra for confirmation.

"Take one of these three times a day," she said, accepting the bottle from Nancy. "But they won't work if you don't change your diet."

Elsie took the bottle with a self-satisfied smile, paid her bill, and left.

"Now she has a new ailment to brag about to Nell and the pills to show for it," Nancy said when she'd left. "Mark my word, Nell will be in wanting the same thing before the week is done."

It was the end of the day, and Nancy and Alexandra were closing the surgery, straightening the room, and preparing to retire to the main part of the house for their evening meal when they heard Zack's frantic barking coming from outside, then Artie and Rob shouting for him to come back.

Alexandra hurried to the surgery door with Nancy close behind her. It was unusual for Zack to bark in such a manner. He usually lay quietly in the hallway while Alexandra saw patients and followed her with devotion as she rode Lucy on her rounds to visit those at home. He'd give his single or double bark to signal that visitors had arrived.

As Alexandra opened the door and peered outside, she saw the two boys running along the driveway toward the road. Both stopped as Zack disappeared from view around a curve obscured by brush.

Alexandra and Nancy ran toward the boys. "Artie! Rob!" Alexandra called. "What's happened to Zack? Where is he going?"

"Seen something, 'e did," Rob shouted.

"What did he see?" Nancy called as she and Alexandra closed the distance between themselves and the boys.

"Not sure." Rob was scanning the road with his eyes, searching for Zack.

"Somethin' scary," Artie said. The little boy was by now hurrying toward Nancy and Alexandra.

"Zack sounded more agitated than scared," Alexandra said, putting her arm around Artie's thin shoulders.

"I think 'e seen that horseman," Artie said, edging closer.

"Horseman?" Nancy asked.

"You know. The one they's all talkin' about in town. The one what rides out to that place they call a temple."

"Oh, Artie," Alexandra said. "That horseman isn't real."

"I knows that," Artie replied. "That's what makes 'im so scary."

Chapter 5

It was neither Artie's fear nor her patients cranky moods that kept Alexandra awake that night. It was Charlotte Malcolm going into labor.

Charlotte was practically a child herself—no more than fifteen years old—and her husband, Samuel, was only two or three years older than Charlotte. When he arrived at the surgery door, he was pale and could hardly speak.

"You must come with me, Nancy," Alexandra called out, though Nancy had already donned her cloak and bonnet by the time the words were out of her mouth. Within a few minutes they were on their way to the small cottage where the young couple lived as they worked the farmland belonging to Nicholas Forsythe, the sixth Earl of Dunsford. Nancy rode behind young Samuel on his horse while Alexandra rode Lucy.

They could hear Charlotte's screams long before they reached the door. As soon as Alexandra and Nancy entered, they both saw Charlotte writhing on the bed.

"You never should have left her alone!" Nancy scolded Samuel. "You should have stopped at a neighbor's place on your way to the surgery and asked someone to stay with her."

White-faced and trembling, Samuel had retreated to a corner and made no indication that he'd heard Nancy's reprimand.

"There's water in the kettle," Alexandra said, directing her comments to Nancy. "I'll wash up first, then you."

Alexandra did her best to calm the screaming girl so she could examine her, but Charlotte, almost as big and robust as her young husband, was proving difficult to handle.

"Samuel, I'll need your help," Alexandra called over her shoulder. "Nancy, we're going to need—" Nancy, with her hands still dripping from the quick wash, clamped a mask soaked in chloroform on Charlotte's face, calming her enough for Alexandra to force her on her back in order to examine her pelvic area. Samuel had not moved from his corner, but they had managed without his help. It took only a few more seconds for Alexandra's prodding to confirm what she had feared. "Breech!" she said in a clipped tone to Nancy.

"God help us!" Nancy said.

"What?" Samuel asked. "What's that mean?"

"Coming out feet first," Nancy said. "Now stay quiet while we try to save her." She had opened both of the emergency medical bags they brought and was pulling out instruments to be doused with an antiseptic solution of carbolic acid. Next she set up a Lister machine, which Alexandra had recently purchased at great expense. The machine, invented by Dr. Joseph Lister, was small and could be mounted on a table as it sprayed a carbolic acid solution over the patient during the surgical procedure. Nancy would have to interrupt her other duties periodically in order to turn the crank to allow the solution to be sprayed over Charlotte's body.

"Is she passed out?" Samuel asked. "Did ye poison 'er?"

"Sleeping," Alexandra said. She didn't have time to explain to him how anesthesia worked and that Queen Victoria's personal decision to use chloroform during childbirth had helped spread its use to many women in the realm. "Help me move her to the table."

Samuel seemed grateful to have something to do. Nancy had already wiped the table with the carbolic acid, and Alexandra took a swath of gauze, doused it in the liquid, and began to bath Charlotte's stomach while Nancy returned to the chloroform mask to try to maintain the delicate balance of giving enough to keep Charlotte unconscious but not enough to kill her.

Alexandra made her first cut, incising Charlotte's mid-section and into the uterus, extending the lengthwise incision with blunt pressure. Behind her, she heard a thump. It was loud enough and startling enough to make her turn around. Samuel was lying prone on the floor. She and Nancy exchanged a glance, but neither stopped what she was doing to attend to him.

When the incision through the uterus was complete, Alexandra grasped the blood-covered male infant and removed him first then the placenta. After she snipped the umbilical cord, she forced her finger down the baby's throat to remove any debris and to make him cry. Charlotte was breathing shallow breaths and moaning, but a brief nod of Nancy's head told Alexandra that, so far, the girl was in at least satisfactory condition. Nancy left her position at Charlotte's head long enough to take the infant boy and clean him.

Samuel groaned and rubbed his head as he pulled himself up to a sitting position. "What?" he said again.

"You have a son," Alexandra said, not adding that there was still danger of Charlotte bleeding to death.

Samuel staggered toward Alexandra and his wife. "I have a. . . ." He took one look at the gaping wound and saw Alexandra insert the cat-gut threaded needle in his wife's flesh and slumped to the floor again.

"Never should have let him stay in the first place," Nancy said, stepping over him with the baby, wrapped in a cloth and tucked into the crook of her arm, as she made her way back to attend to the ether mask.

"There wasn't much time to dispatch him," Alexandra said.

Nancy nodded at the new mother. "How is she?"

"I don't know," Alexandra said. "We can only hope, but there's always so much blood loss with a Cesarean birth. So much risk of infection, even when we use the carbolic acid."

Alexandra finished closing the womb, and Nancy gave Samuel a quick whiff of smelling salts before ordering him outside until he was called.

"Is they all right? The two of 'em?" he asked in a weak voice.

"Pray that they are, Sam," Nancy said. "'Twill give you something to do while you wait." She gave him a shove outside and closed the door then set about cleaning the room of the blood and debris the procedure and created. Alexandra remained by Charlotte's side where she still lay on the table. It was too early to move her, and she wanted to make sure the girl was able to awaken. Nancy alternately bathed the girl's face and tried to soothe the crying infant, who, by now, had been placed in a homemade cradle. Alexandra found that Charlotte's pulse was erratic, and she was having a difficult time awakening from the anesthesia. Meanwhile, the baby continued to cry.

"What's wrong with it?" Samuel shouted through the closed door. "What are you doing to it?"

"He's hungry," Nancy snapped at him. "And he's not an *it*. He's a boy. Your son. Now be quiet! We're busy."

"Let him in," Alexandra said. "This is going to be a long night. He should be by her side if she passes."

Nancy hesitated slightly before she nodded and opened the door. "Come in," she said.

Samuel took a reluctant step inside the door and glanced at his wife. "She's dead, ain't she?"

"She's not dead," Nancy said, "but she's doing poorly. You've got to be strong. She needs you now."

Still pale and trembling, Samuel nodded, and moved to the table. He seemed not to know what to do with himself at first, but he picked up one of Charlotte's limp hands. Nancy picked up the baby and held him, swaying back and forth to quiet him. Alexandra took over the job of bathing Charlotte's face until she was awake enough to attempt to nurse the baby.

When the pale light of dawn crept across the sea-side village, Alexandra had Samuel help her move Charlotte to the bed then sent him to fetch Wilma Beaty to stay with Charlotte and the baby so she and Nancy could return home to their other duties. Wilma knew well what needed to be done, and without a word, she set about trying to spoon some of the broth she'd brought into Charlotte's mouth. When Nancy and Alexandra left at last, Charlotte, weak from loss of blood, still had not fully awakened, and Samuel was sound asleep on the floor next to her bed.

Alexandra would have to forego her morning rounds, and she was thankful none of the patients who were homebound were in critical need of her. She and Nancy had hoped for a short nap before patients began to show up at the surgery door. That was not to be, however, and it was past noon before Alexandra could get away to visit Judith Payne again.

The young woman was working in her and looked up when she heard Alexandra approaching on Lucy. Leaning on her garden hoe, she gave Alexandra a brief nod. There was no smile, however, and her expression was blank

"Good afternoon, Judith," Alexandra said.

Judith made no response.

Alexandra dismounted and took a step toward the young woman. "I meant to stop by earlier, but I was called away."

There was still no response from Judith.

"I didn't have time to tell you yesterday that I was unable to speak to the Constable Snow. It seems he's left the village for some reason."

"I know," Judith said and nothing more.

"According to the note he left on his door, there is to be a deputy in charge. Perhaps I could bring him here so you can tell him your story."

"No," Judith said, breaking her silence at last. "I've changed my mind about that."

"Judith. . . ."

" It's because I'm afraid. I should never have mentioned it. Not even to you. Please don't betray me." Her voice trembled even more.

"Of course I won't betray you, Judith, but if your father is a murderer as you say, it's difficult for me to understand why you wouldn't want him arrested."

"I'm protecting myself. You see what he's capable of."

"If you truly believe he may harm you, that's all the more the reason that you should inform the authorities," Alexandra said. "If what you believe about your father is true, he should be arrested."

"And if he learns I'm the one who set them on him, he'd come for me."

"Your father need not know you spoke to the deputy. I believe I can assure you of that."

Judith was silent for a moment. "Are you certain no one will know?"

"Yes, Alexandra said. "I can arrange it so no one will know. You will come to my house on the pretext of visiting the surgery. I will arrange for you to talk to the deputy, or the constable if he has returned."

"If any of your patients see me there when the constable or his deputy is present, word is certain to get back to my father."

"Please trust me," Alexandra said.

Judith was silent for another long moment. "All right," she said finally. "I will do it if I have your word."

Alexandra took her hand in both of hers in a gesture of warmth and reassurance. "Of course," she said.

Now she must set things in action. She would need cooperation from the constable's office. She was certain it would be more effective to deal with Snow himself than with a deputy. She would enlist the aid of the sixth Earl of Dunsford to locate him.

Chapter 6

Nicholas Forsythe, sixth Earl of Dunsford, was not at home at his country estate, Montmarsh, outside of Newton-upon-Sea. He did not reside there permanently, as might be expected of him. Instead, he spent a great deal of his time in London, where he still maintained his practice as a barrister, a source of considerable chagrin and embarrassment to his mother, Lady Anne Forsythe. To her, his law practice was unbearably middle-class, and she'd greatly prefer that her son concentrate on his estate and his position in the House of Lords. She wanted him to marry a suitable woman and live the life that was expected of him at Montmarsh as Lord Dunsford. In her mind, the only reason to be thankful that he spent as little time at Montmarsh as he did was that it meant he saw less of Alexandra Gladstone. He seemed not to care at all that she was entirely unacceptable.

As for Alexandra, while unable to deny to herself that she found Lord Dunsford attractive in more ways than one, she was determined that nothing of a romantic nature would ever develop between them. Her reasons were similar to those of Lady Forsythe's. The difference in their class over-complicated any relationship.

She also knew that Lord Dunsford was not at Montmarsh. In spite of his attempts to slip in and out unseen, everyone in the parish knew when he was or was not residing in his country house. For that reason, Alexandra didn't bother to ride Lucy out to the estate but stopped at the telegraph office at the train station   She sent him a brief wire telling him she believed Constable Snow to be in London since it was his habit to make frequent visits to the city, and she asked his help in locating him. Lord Dunsford, by virtue of his law practice as well as his seat in the House of Lords, had remarkable means and connections to accomplish any number of seemingly impossible tasks.

As soon as the wire was sent, she told Michael Gray, the telegraph man, that she expected a reply that could be delivered to her home where she would be busy in the surgery. Mr. Gray was a man in his late thirties with light colored hair and features so unremarkable they would be difficult to describe. He reminded Alexandra of a nondescript drawing of a human figure in one of her medical texts. He was impeccably professional in his work in that he never commented on any message he translated from the electronic *click-clack* of his machine. The end result was that it made his personality appear as bland as his looks.

Alexandra went back to her surgery to see patients, expecting to be interrupted at any time by one of the boys Mr. Gray hired as runners to deliver telegrams. When the day ended, and she still had received no word from Lord Dunsford, she could only assume he was traveling and had never received her message.

Zack, who had a way of sensing when something was wrong, emitted a soft, whining growl as he stood in front of her while she sat in a chair with a book and tried to relax in the parlor.

"Something troubling you, Miss Alex?" Nancy asked. She had never called her mistress Miss Gladstone or Dr. Gladstone, or even Miss Alexandra. She'd never lost the habit she'd developed when they were children and playmates.

"What makes you think there's something—"

"No need to deny it, miss." Nancy interrupted.

Alexandra sighed audibly. "No, I suppose not," she said and told Nancy about her conversation with Judith. "I thought if I could contact Nicholas. . . .I should say, Lord Dunsford-- he could help me find Constable Snow so I could arrange a secret meeting between the constable and Judith. It's important that the entire matter be handled with great discretion."

"Find Constable Snow!" Nancy sounded indignant. "He's always running off to London, and I suspect he doesn't want to be found. He has a secret life there, and you can be sure it involves a woman. But there's more to it this time. He doesn't usually leave in the middle of trouble in the village."

"I'm not concerned with his secret life, if indeed there is one. I'm seeking his help."

"Left at a bad time, I'd say."

"I agree, he's never left so suddenly," Alexandra mused. "And he always gives the town notice that he'll be away for a day."

"Suspicious, if you ask me."

"You're still trying to implicate him in the murders."

"Of course not. Got no proof, now do I? All I can say is I just have a caution. . . ." Nancy let her voice trail off.

Alexandra gave her a concerned look. However, she'd learned long ago not to dismiss Nancy's "cautions." All too often she'd had a prescience about something amiss that turned out to be valid. She didn't want to think that Constable Snow was in any way connected to the murders as Nancy had hinted earlier..

"I suppose he left Daniel Poole in charge as the deputy, just as he always does," Nancy said.

"That's likely," Alexandra agreed. "I suppose I could ask Deputy Poole to come here to meet Judith, if all else fails.

"Excuse me, miss, but I have to say, Miss Payne is right when she says every patient who came to the clinic will know both of them were here. Newton's the kind of town where everyone knows everyone else's affairs and all their comings and goings, and gossip spreads fast. I wouldn't rely on it not getting back to her father, even if he is in Foulness."

"If only Nicholas were here. . ." Alexandra regretted her words as soon as she spoke.

"Don't see how His Lordship could help." Nancy sounded more than a little disdainful.

Alexandra was silent for a moment. "He owns a carriage—a truly fine one he uses when he travels up from London," she said, thinking aloud.

Nancy gave her a confused and questioning look. "True, he has a fine carriage, but 'tis not relevant to the problem if you ask me."

"He almost always comes here to my house when he travels up to Montmarsh from London." By this time Zack had relaxed and was resting his head on Alexandra's knee.

"'Tis true, Nancy agreed. "Everyone knows that's because he's sweet on you. Even you know that, I dare say."

"The reason he comes here is irrelevant. The point is, no one will consider it out of the ordinary," Alexandra said. Much to her chagrin, she knew she was blushing, but she carried on. "So if Judith is here, he can spirit her away, hiding under a blanket perhaps, in his carriage, and—"

"And you think no one will see her leave?" Nancy asked, her voice full of doubt.

"We can arrange that somehow, I expect."

"We? You're going to involve me? Forgive me, miss, but I don't think I—"

"Oh stop it, Nancy. You're always up for something tricky and devious."

Nancy hesitated for a moment. "Well. . . . Perhaps you're right, but it's not like *you* to be tricky and devious."

"You've corrupted me, Nancy," Alexandra said and grinned.

Nancy frowned. "Are you sure you've thought this through completely? Where's Lord Dunsford going to take her once he has her hidden in a blanket? To the constable's office? Someone will see her there."

"I think he should take her to Montmarsh," Alexandra said, referring to the earl's large country estate. "It shouldn't be too hard to spirit her into the house. It has so many doors, you know, including one that's more or less hidden from view that leads down to the kitchen and servants' quarters."

"Which you've used to your advantage on another occasion," Nancy said, her eyes flashing mischief.

Alexandra blushed. "That's neither here nor there, Nancy."

"More to the point," Nancy said, enjoying herself, "is why take her to Montmarsh?"

"Constable Snow, if he's back, can come later, or the deputy if need be, and Judith can tell him her story," Alexandra said. "It's certainly not unusual for the constable to meet with Lord Dunsford when he's here. There's always business relating to the assizes or the county elections, or issues to present to Parliament. Any number of things."

"Oh my! I see I've taught you well," Nancy said. "You've become quite devious. Still, I think your plan is a bit farfetched, and I'd be careful about telling the constable too much."

Alexandra did her best to ignore Nancy and to concentrate on her reading, but it was a futile attempt. She put her book aside and, telling Nancy she was going to retire, started up the stairs to her bedroom. That's when Zack set up a frenzied angry bark, alternating with a menacing growl.

Alexandra stopped on her way up the stairs and looked down at Nancy who was trying to quiet Zack. "There's someone out there," Alexandra said, hurrying down. "Something must have happened to Charlotte. Tell the boys to saddle Lucy and—"

"No need for that," Nancy said, peeking out of a front window, "Speak of the devil."

"The devil?" Alexandra picked up her medical bag and was searching for her cloak.

"Lord Dunsford."

"He's here?" Alexandra was unable to keep the excitement out of her voice. "I was afraid he was traveling and wouldn't get the wire."

Nancy had already started to the door. "I'll wager he hasn't eaten, and we'll have to have a try at filling his belly."

When an urgent knock sounded at the door, Zack's barking stopped. But his low growl sounded even more menacing. "Hush now, Zack," Nancy said. "He's not here to take her away from you." Nancy's theory was that Zack, who treated all others, friends and strangers alike, with the happy eagerness of a puppy, was particularly jealous of Lord Dunsford and disliked him because of his attraction to Alexandra.

"Nicholas!" Alexandra's heartbeat quickened. "I really didn't expect you to come. I only meant to ask you to help me find--"

"I took the late train," Nicholas said, shucking off his coat. "Was almost the only person to board, but I couldn't get away any sooner." He was eyeing the enormous dog with caution as Alexandra forced Zack away from her guest and made him sit.

"You said you needed to consult with me. Is something wrong?" Nicholas asked, absently handing his coat to Nancy.

"I thought you'd telegraph a reply," Alexandra said, still a bit stunned. "I didn't expect you to come so quickly."

"You know I'm always looking for an excuse to come back to Montmarsh. More and more lately, I'm thinking of making it my permanent home, you know."

Alexandra was even more surprised. "You'd give up your practice as a barrister?"

"I could always be available, couldn't I? If a good case should arise, I mean." Nicholas took a seat as far away from Zack as possible.

"I'm sure I don't know about such things," Alexandra said, "but my guess is it would make Lady Forsythe happy if you gave up practicing law."

"I can assure you my motive isn't to please MaMa. Oh, what have we here?" Nicholas said as Nancy reappeared, bearing a tray.

"I knew you'd be hungry," Nancy said, setting the tray on a table next to Nicholas' chair. "We had a bit of boiled beef and a hasty pudding with treacle."

"Aw, Nancy, your cooking is one of the many reasons I'm contemplating making Montmarsh and Newton-upon-Sea my permanent home."

Nancy rolled her eyes and moved toward the hallway that led out to the kitchen. She'd never been known as a good cook, and she was certain the earl was only trying to flatter her. Or tease her. She didn't leave the room entirely, however. Alexandra and Nicholas both knew she would be far too interested in what they had to say to venture too far. Zack, in the meantime, had not taken his eyes off Nicholas.

"Now, what's this about Constable Snow? Disappeared, has he?" Nicholas touched a napkin to his mouth and pulled his foot in a bit closer, imagining Zack had his eye on it.

Alexandra took notice. "Nancy, would you remove Zack from the room, please? I fear his presence with Lord Dunsford's could interfere with his digestion. You've heard the story, so you won't be missing anything."

"Of course, miss," Nancy said, moving toward Zack to urge him out of the room." And as for my missing anything, you know I'm not in the habit of eavesdropping." She managed a hurt look on her face.

"Thank you, Nancy," Nicholas said to her back as she led Zack away. "The beast does have a way of making me uncomfortable." Turning to Alexandra, he said, "Now about your request. . . ."

Before Alexandra had finished telling Nicholas about Judith's suspicion about her father and her fear of him, she saw Nancy had moved with Zack within her own hearing range of their conversation. Alexandra continued nonetheless, explaining her strategy.

"My dear Alexandra, that is a rather convoluted scheme you've come up with," Nicholas said when she'd told him her plan to ferry Judith away in his carriage and take her to Montmarsh for a meeting with the constable or deputy.

"I'm afraid Nancy agrees with you that it's somewhat contrived," Alexandra said with a glance toward her maid who was back in the hallway trying to appear not to be listening. "I am, of course, open to a better idea," she added, a tinge of hope in her voice.

"Well, I certainly agree with you that Miss Payne must share her suspicion with the authorities," Nicholas said, "and I shall give it some thought as to how we can accommodate her. Shall I contact you first thing in the morning? I'm sure I'll have it all worked out by then."

"You're very kind, Nicholas. I knew I could count on you," Alexandra said, "and yes, please do let me know as early as possible. Poor Judith is simply tormented by all of this. If you could come by here before eight in the morning before my rounds, I would be able to stop by her house. It will give her a great deal of reassurance, I'm quite certain."

"Before eight, you say?"

Alexandra noted the look on Nicholas' face. It was nothing less than consternation. "Is that too early, my lord?"

"Too early? Of course not," Nicholas said, sounding flustered in spite of himself. "I'm quite used to rising early."

"Of course, my lord. Forgive me if I offended you."

Nicholas laughed. "When you start addressing me as *my lord*, there is almost always trouble ahead."

"I certainly hope not," Alexandra said.

"Nevertheless, I think it best we both get a good night's sleep so we can be effective with the plan I devise," Nicholas said, standing.

"You're right, of course," Alexandra said. "Nancy, fetch Lord Dunsford's coat, please?"

Nancy appeared almost instantly, holding the coat. "Thank you, Nancy," Nicholas said. "Always good to be back in Newton-upon-Sea where everything runs so smoothly." He slipped an arm into a sleeve. "Oh, and by the way," he said as Nancy helped him into the other sleeve, "I saw the most extraordinary thing as I was driving the through the village."

"Oh?" Alexandra said, and what was that?"

"A horseman. Not that it's odd to see a horseman in the village, but this one appeared to be in costume, dressed as a knight. I might even say as a Templar. He had that red cross on his breast front."

Chapter 7

"At least I can take some measure of comfort in thinking I'm not hallucinating," Nicholas said when Alexandra told him Hannibal Talbot had recently seen a horseman dressed as a Templar Knight. They were still standing near the doorway as Nicholas prepared to leave.

"Another of my patients, Mrs. Fontaine, also mentioned something about a horseman. I'm not sure what it is all about, but it's more than a little odd," Alexandra said.

Nicholas nodded. "Indeed. But no more so than Constable Snow disappearing in the middle of a murder investigation."

"I couldn't agree with you more," Alexandra said. "Some believe he's in London. I hoped you could use your influence and contacts to locate him."

"I'll do all I can. I shall send a telegram to a captain I know at Scotland Yard."

"Thank you, Nicholas," Alexandra said. "In the meantime, we can only hope that the deputy he left in charge is competent to handle all that's going on here at the moment."

"Do you know the chap?" Nicholas asked.

"The constable usually calls upon Daniel Poole, but I'm afraid I don't know him terribly well. I believe he started out to be an articled clerk for one of the solicitors here but never finished his apprenticeship. I'm not certain why he didn't complete the endeavor, but—"

Alexandra was interrupted by a dramatic cough from Nancy.

"Is that a signal that you have something to add to the conversation?" Nicholas asked with a playful look on his face.

"Well, since you asked, my lord," Nancy said, "he's a lazy lout. Smart enough to be a law clerk, I'd guess, but a bit of a laggard. That's why he never finished the apprenticeship."

"Hmm," Nicholas said.

"It's true, he moves around from job to job. Doesn't seem to hang onto anything for long," Alexandra agreed.

"And this is the man you want me to spirit the young woman away to speak with." Nicholas sounded doubtful.

"Unless you can think of a better idea," Alexandra said. "Or unless you can quickly locate Constable Snow."

"As I said, I'll give the matter some thought," Nicholas said. "And you can rest assured I'll send that telegram to Captain Mitchell at Scotland Yard immediately. I'll stop by the telegraph office when I leave here." He glanced at Nancy and saw her intense expression. "Well, Nancy, what do you make of all of this. The horseman, the murders?"

"Me?" Nancy said, pretending surprise. "What would I know of any such goings on? Freemasons, Knights Templar, a father angry enough at his daughter to kill her suitors? None of that's within the realm of my small world."

"I see," Nicholas said.

"Well now that you mention it, I suppose it wouldn't hurt to find out about that horseman you claim you saw, would it?" Nancy said.

"Perhaps you're right," Nicholas told her. "But how would one go about doing that?"

"I'm not the one to come up with an elaborate plan, you know, me being a simple maid-of-all-work."

"Oh, you're far from simple, Nancy old girl."

"Nevertheless, such things are out of my purview."

"Of course." Nicholas glanced at Zack, who was standing at attention, apparently eager for the earl to leave. Nicholas turned his eyes back to Nancy. "If those things *were* within your purview, what would you say would be the best approach to finding out who this horseman is and what his motive is?"

"Why I watch the Temple of the Ninth Daughter, of course," Nancy said without hesitating. "That's where most of the sightings have been. I'd watch to see when the horseman shows up then follow him. He's bound to ride home eventually, isn't he?"

"Oh, you are undoubtedly right," Nicholas said.

"But don't go asking me to come up with any such hare-brained scheme. I'll have no part of such things."

"Of course not. I certainly wouldn't expect you to." Nicholas paused briefly. "If one were to follow the rider home, as you mentioned, one would assume he is from Newton, I suppose, or somewhere near here."

"Certainly he's from around here. How else would he be able to show up so frequently?" Nancy said.

When Nicholas returned the next day and relayed the plan he had devised to have Judith meet, unseen, with law enforcement, Alexandra was disappointed.

"It sounds rather like the same thing I suggested," Alexandra said.

"It's hard to improve upon perfection," Nicholas said.. "Except I had to work at the details and arrange everything."

"I see," Alexandra said.

"Everything," Nicholas said, "down to the scheduled arrival of Deputy Poole, ostensibly to speak with me on matters pertaining to the county and Parliament. I must admit, however, it did take some persuading to get the chap to agree to meet with me."

"I should have thought he would be eager to have such an important meeting," Alexandra said.

Nicholas shook his head. "Quite the contrary. Said he didn't feel qualified for a discussion of that nature and insisted I wait until a constable is in office."

"That's an odd way of putting it," Alexandra said. "One would think he'd say something about waiting until Constable Snow returns. Waiting until a constable is in office makes it sound as if he doesn't expect Constable Snow to return."

"'Tis beginning to look as if that's the case," Nancy said. She had just entered the parlor where Alexandra was speaking with Nicholas.

"Not like you to have such a negative attitude, Nancy," Nicholas said. "I hope you're not equally as doubtful of the plan."

"We shall see," Nancy said. "Perhaps it will work. Stranger things have happened."

Alexandra was growing more and more uneasy about the matter.

"Are we to assume you've had no response to the telegram you sent to Scotland Yard?"

Nicholas shook his head. "None. Perhaps later today. Have to give the fellows a little time, you know."

That evening, Nicholas returned as planned. A few minutes later, Nancy brought Judith to him from where she waited in the kitchen.

Nicholas greeted her with a little bow and said, "Miss Payne, I presume."

"My lord," she answered. Her voice was barely audible.

With the aid of Artie and Rob, Judith was whisked to the carriage under the cover of night and positioned so that she could be hidden under a dark blanket. Nicholas then escorted Alexandra to the carriage so that, in the unlikely event that anyone was watching, it would appear that his driver was taking the two of them for an evening drive.

The driver left Alexandra and Lord Dunsford at the front door, and the plan seemed to be going well until he made his way to the kitchen entrance in the back where Judith was to be moved, once again under cover of darkness, into the house. The deputy had not yet arrived, but Alexandra was sitting in the large receiving room with Nicholas, waiting for both Judith and Deputy Poole when, Stokes, the butler, appeared at the door with the driver behind him.

"Osmond wishes to speak with my lord," Stokes said.

"Come in, Osmond." Nicholas stood to greet the driver.

"Forgive the intrusion, my lord," the driver said, "but the young lady is refusing to leave the carriage."

Nicholas frowned. "I don't understand. Why would she refuse to leave the carriage?"

"Says she's afraid, my lord."

"Afraid? Afraid of what?"

"I'm sure I don't know, but she refuses to move from the carriage."

"I'll speak to her." Alexandra maneuvered her way around both Nicholas and the driver. When she'd hurried through the house and out the door, she found Judith just as they'd left her, huddled on the floor of the carriage with the dark blanket still draped over her head and shoulders.

"Judith," Alexandra said, going to her, "there's no need to be frightened."

"You're wrong. There is every need to be."

"You're safe here. I can assure you of that."

"I wish I could believe that." Judith's voice trembled as she spoke. "But I can't. Already someone else knows I'm here—the carriage driver. Next, my father will find out what I've done, and he'll have no mercy on me."

"My dear Judith, you must come inside. Leaving yourself exposed out here in the carriage offers far more opportunity for someone to discover you. You must be strong and stick to your convictions. As strong as any man. No, as strong as any woman."

For a moment Judith didn't speak, but Alexandra saw that she had persuaded her when she slipped the blanket from her head and stood up in a crouched position as if she were trying to make herself smaller. Alexandra led her into the house and all the way to the parlor where Nicholas waited. He'd had tea as well as brandy brought in and offered it to both of them. Alexandra accepted a cup of tea while Judith asked for brandy. Her hands shook as she held the glass.

"I can't imagine why Deputy Poole hasn't arrived," Nicholas said.

"Perhaps he's not coming," Judith said. "Perhaps this meeting was not meant to be."

"I'm afraid I don't believe in predestination," Nicholas said. "If he doesn't show up this time, we'll make it happen eventually."

Judith gave him a troubled look, but before she could respond, Stokes came in with an announcement.

"Deputy Daniel Poole is here to see you, my lord."

"Of course," Nicholas said. "Show him in."

Deputy Poole was a short, stocky man, the exact opposite of the tall, slender Constable Snow. He lacked Snow's taciturn aloofness as well and entered the room appearing awkward and uncomfortable. He seemed surprised, perhaps even alarmed, to see the two women in the room with Lord Dunsford.

"Oh!" he said, twisting his cap in his hands.

"Dr. Alexandra Gladstone, Miss Judith Payne, may I present Deputy Daniel Poole," Nicholas said.

"How do you do," Alexandra said.

Judith didn't speak, and Deputy Poole seemed equally dumbstruck.

"Please have a seat, Deputy Poole," Nicholas said, pointing to a chair. "The ladies have something to discuss with you."

"I'm not up to this, my lord." Poole looked even more uncomfortable than he had when he'd first arrived. "I'm just filling in 'til a constable gets here. I told you, I know nothing of the business of Parliament."

"Yes, you made that same confession to me earlier, and I apologize for insisting that you come anyway. You'll be relieved to learn that the matter to be discussed has nothing to do with the business of Parliament after all," Nicholas said.

Deputy Poole's discomfort was growing incrementally, and Alexandra noticed that Judith's face had become alarmingly white. She managed only a slight flush when she realized everyone was looking at her.

"Tell the deputy what you told us," Nicholas prompted.

Judith hesitated a little longer before she managed to speak. "I. . .I know who killed those men."

Deputy Poole's eyes widened. "What men?"

The deputy's response had surprised and confused everyone, but none more than Judith. She glanced first at Alexandra and the Nicholas before she answered in an uncertain tone, "The men of the brotherhood. The Freemasons."

"You're speaking of Jeremy Fitzsimmons and Saul Mayhew?" Poole asked.

Judith gave the other two in the room another uncertain glance and said, "Of course."

"What makes you think they were murdered?"

Judith looked as if she might burst into tears. "Why, because. . .because everyone knows they were. The way they died, everyone says it must have been murder."

"It is simply not true that everyone knows the men were murdered," Poole said, his face flushing to an unattractive hue. "I for one, know no such thing. Since the investigation isn't complete, no conclusions have been made on the part of law enforcement."

"But you should know! It was my father who killed them." Judith had stood and all but shouted her words, growing more and more agitated by the second.

"Your father?" Poole asked. "You have some reason to be so angry with your father that you would accuse him of murder?"

"He. . .he. . . ." Judith collapsed to the floor, and Alexandra rushed to her side.

"My medical bag is with my cloak. Fetch it now!" Alexandra said, speaking to both Nicholas and the deputy. "I'll need a basin of water and a cloth!"

Nicholas produced the bag, and Stokes showed up in short order with a basin of water and a cloth. Alexandra pulled a vial of smelling salts from her bag to pass under Judith's nose.

"I say, why are you so reluctant to believe the young woman?" Nicholas asked with a sharp hint of anger in his voice. "I should think you'd be glad for any help you can get in this matter."

"I'm quite used to dealing with overwrought young women, my lord," Poole said. "I have three sisters, and I know how the feminine disposition affects their thinking."

Alexandra snapped at Poole over her shoulder while she continued to work with Judith. "This has nothing to do with a feminine disposition, whatever that is. Don't dismiss her statement as hysteria."

"Forgive me, Dr. Gladstone, but you have no idea how much hysteria I've had to deal with since the constable up and left. There's that horseman for one thing, and—"

"I can attest with certainty that the horseman exists," Nicholas said. "I've seen him with my own eyes."

"Yes, my lord. I've seen him myself," Poole said.

Alexandra was in the process of helping Judith to a sofa to help her lie down, but she glanced at Poole in surprise.

Nicholas spoke, voicing his own surprise. "You've seen him? Explain yourself, Poole."

Poole shrugged. "There's nothing to explain, is there, my lord? I've seen him, and I can't say for certain who it might be or why he might be dressed in that garb, but I have reason to believe 'tis the constable himself."

"Good God, man!" Nicholas said.

"Constable Snow?" Alexandra said at the same time.

Poole's face took on a sanctimonious expression. "Can't say more. This is police business."

"Police business be damned!" Nicholas said. "You are accusing the man in charge of law enforcement in this village of frightening people by riding around at night dressed as a Templar Knight."

"Didn't say he was purposely frightening anybody. Just said it looks like the constable to me."

By this time Alexandra had Judith sitting upright and was wiping her face with a damp cloth. "What possible motive would Constable Snow have for doing that?" Alexandra asked.

"I wouldn't be knowing that, now would I, miss?" Poole said.

"This unknown rider only *looks like* Snow in your opinion. Not very substantial, would you say?" Nicholas said.

Poole shrugged. "Same slight build, same horse."

"Same horse?" Alexandra asked. "Do you agree, Lord Dunsford? That the rider you saw was on a horse that looked like the constable's horse?"

Nicholas shook his head. "I can't say. It was rather dark, don't you know."

"Yes," Judith said, speaking for the first time since she'd fainted. "I've seen it, too. I think it was Constable Snow's horse the man was riding."

Chapter 8

"A waste of time," Alexandra said in response to Nancy's question about the meeting with Deputy Poole. She and Nicholas were in the parlor, which, after the death of her father, had become less formal and more of a drawing room.

"A colossal waste of time," Nicholas said, his arm resting on the white Parian mantelpiece, his elbow dangerously close to a crystal candelabrum that had belonged to Alexandra's mother. "He's inept. Completely uninterested in the situation, if you ask me." Nicholas was keeping a wary eye on Zack, who had just entered the parlor. He had been lounging in the hallway that led to the surgery until he heard Nicholas' voice. "He even voiced an opinion that Constable Snow was the mysterious Templar Knight some of us have seen. Odd, isn't it?"

"I'm not so sure it's odd," Nancy said.

Nicholas straightened. "What do you mean?"

Nancy shrugged. "You have to admit the constable has always been a bit secretive. Well, at least not very forthcoming about his private life. Just a strange bird, all in all, and besides that, I have a caution that something is going on, something unusual."

"You have a caution?" Nicholas said. "I'm afraid I don't understand."

"It's not easy to explain," Nancy said.

"Sometimes Nancy is prescient," Alexandra said.

Nicholas frowned. "Oh come now—"

"You're right, it's probably nothing," Nancy said and quickly changed the subject. "If I may ask, what was Miss Payne's reaction to the meeting with the deputy?" Nancy asked.

"She was as disappointed as Lord Dunsford and I were," Alexandra said. "Deputy Poole seemed to completely dismiss Judith's story."

"Getting back to that so-called Templar," Nicholas said, "Miss Payne and Deputy Poole both believe it's Constable Snow's horse that strange would-be knight is riding."

Alexandra frowned. "It's all a bit far-fetched. Why would someone be riding the constable's horse?"

Nancy made an innocent-sounding cough but said nothing. She was pretending to be busy folding bandages as she relaxed in one of the red velvet chairs next to the fireplace. Zack ambled over to stand next to Alexandra, who sat in a matching chair, his eyes never leaving Nicholas.

"Why, indeed?" Nicholas said. "It's not going to be easy to get to the bottom of any of this."

Nancy made her fake-sounding cough again, a little louder this time.

"We can only hope there are no more deaths," Alexandra said. "We would all feel so much better if the constable. . . ." There was a loud thump and several feet of white bandages unwound as they snaked across the floor. "What *is it,* Nancy? If there's something you must say, then say it."

"Well, I don't mean to be impertinent," Nancy began.

"Of course you do," Alexandra said, "but go on."

"It's just that it seems to me there is a way we could get to the bottom of this--"

"Oh no," Alexandra interrupted her again. "Your idea of spying that you mentioned earlier won't work."

"Excuse me, miss, but—"

"I say, you did mention a plan to watch the temple," Nicholas said. He took a step forward, but backed up again when Zack made a slight move toward him. "What did you have in mind, Nancy?"

"'Tis the obvious solution, if you ask me," Nancy said, clearly eager to have her say. "As I pointed out, this knight, or whatever he is, has been seen several time recently, mostly around the Masonic Temple, which makes sense if you think about it, since people say the Freemasons grew out of the Knights Templar."

"That's never been verified actually," Nicholas said, "but I think I see what you're getting at. Please go on."

"He rides at night, they say," Nancy continued. "I wouldn't know because I've never seen him with my own eyes, but if 'tis true—"

"Of course!" Nicholas said. "I remember your suggestion. We wait at the temple. Undercover, so to speak. Sounds like one of those American novels, but it's brilliant. *You're* brilliant, Nancy, old girl."

Nancy blushed. "As I said, 'tis nothing more than the obvious solution."

"What's not so obvious, however, is that if we do see this so-called knight, how to determine exactly who he is?" Alexandra asked. "Are we going to take this American adventure to the ultimate and shoot him off of his horse so we can see his face?"

"But who's to say we won't recognize him just by seeing him close?" Nicholas said. "I say it's worth a try."

Nancy nodded with an excited look in her eyes and she glanced first at Nicholas and then Alexandra.

"I say we do it," Nicholas said. "I say we start now, while it's good and dark. We can take my carriage, leave it a few yards from the temple, and walk to the building under the cover of darkness. What do you say, Dr. Gladstone?"

"I say you only call me Dr. Gladstone when you're trying to win me over to something, and I might ask why you thought my scheme of getting Judith Payne to your place to talk to the deputy was so far-fetched when it pales in the light of your plan."

"Alexandra, my dear, you obviously need to read the right kind of literature if you want to stay current with this sort of thing," Nicholas said/

A breeze had blown a thin veil of fog in from the sea, rendering what might have been a bright half-moon pale and weary-looking. The air felt damp, and, if it not quite cold, it was uncomfortably cool. The three would-be spies walked a few yards from where Nicholas had left his carriage, which he'd driven himself, not wanting to involve a driver in their scheme. They moved toward the Temple of the Ninth Daughter which looked like a hovering monster in the hazy darkness. The tall pillars in front appeared as enormous teeth, and open-mouthed lions guarded each side of the opening. A growth of brush and trees around the building offered cover to the three of them as they huddled together, communicating with one another only with gestures.

Finally, after what she judged to be near half an hour, Alexandra broke the silence with a whisper. "This is futile and ridiculous."

"Shhh," Nicholas said, putting a finger to his lips.

Nancy said nothing and sat so still Alexandra was astounded at her fortitude and patience. Nicholas was the first, after several more minutes, to show signs of restlessness. He bobbed up several times to peer over the tops of the brush that obscured them and finally stood upright, searching all around in the dim light.

"Sit down, or you'll be seen," Alexandra whispered.

"Seen by whom?" Nicholas whispered in response. "There's no one around. The horseman isn't riding tonight."

Nancy rolled her shoulders as if sitting still for so long had made them ache.

"I feel ridiculous," Alexandra muttered. "We should leave."

This time Nancy nodded, and after a brief pause, Nicholas sighed and stood up. Nancy and Alexandra stood as well, and almost immediately something hovered over them, glowing white in the sickly light of the partially obscured moon. The specter was accompanied by a sweet smell. In the same instant, Alexandra looked up into the flaring nostrils of a white horse and then raised her gaze higher to see that the deathly glow came from the white tunic the rider wore. It was making a weak reflection of the moonlight. Before the rider turned his horse and rode away at a fast gallop, she saw the red cross sewn on the breast of the tunic. It was the traditional dress of the Knights Templar. All three of them ran toward the carriage.

"'Twas no ghost we saw. I take some comfort in that," Nancy said when they were safely back in the carriage. "'Twas a flesh and blood human."

"An altogether unnerving experience, nevertheless," Nicholas added. "And he got away so quickly, it's too late to follow him."

"Can either of you say whether or not the horse was Constable Snow's?" Alexandra asked.

"All I can say is the horse was white," Nancy said. "Same color as the one the constable rides."

"I'm afraid I'd never be able to swear under oath to anything other than the color of the animal myself," Nicholas said. "And you're right, Alexandra. We don't know any more than we did before. It seems every turn we take leads to a dead end."

"Did you notice the oddly sweet smell?" Alexandra asked.

"Nothing odd about it. Just the usual horse smell," Nancy said.

"I have to agree," Nicholas said. "No odd smell, just bloody frightening."

"Frightening, yes," Alexandra agreed. "But there was that odor. . . . I can't quite identify it."

"It means there's going to be another death." Nancy's voice was heavy with fear and foreboding. Each time someone sees the horseman, someone dies."

It was the next morning when Alexandra had started her rounds to see homebound patients that Nancy's prediction was confirmed. When she stopped by Olive Fontaine's home to make sure she was safe and well, she learned the news.

"That young man, the Poole boy," Mrs. Fontaine said. "I'm told he has passed on." Tears rimmed her eyes. "Such a young man. Knew his grandparents years ago."

Alexandra was alarmed. "Do you mean Deputy Daniel Poole?"

Mrs. Fontaine nodded and stroked the white Persian cat that had just jumped into her lap. "Died right in front of his house. Nell Stillwell was the one who found him when she went to deliver a sausage to young Poole's neighbor. You know, Mrs. Ives next door, the one who can't walk well enough to do her own shopping."

"Why wasn't I sent for?" Alexandra was gripped by a sense of unease. With Constable Snow gone and now the deputy dead, the parish could descend into chaos.

"Why you were sent for, my dear," Mrs. Fontaine said. "Nell stopped by here to deliver my own sausage. She was in and out like a frightened cat. Said she was on her way to fetch you."

Alexandra, who had not had time even to put down her bag, turned back to Mrs. Fontaine's front door. "Unless you're in need of anything, I'd best be on my way to Mr. Poole's home," she said.

"I need nothing. Please go," Mrs. Fontaine said. "Although, it's too late, of course. Nell says the poor boy obviously died of an apoplexy. He's young for that, now isn't he? Still, you'd best be gone. It will give the village some comfort to think someone is in charge. Oh, and there's one more thing," Mrs. Fontaine said just as Alexandra turned away. "Poor Danny was wearing his Masonic apron. Nell said there was a spot of blood on it."

When Alexandra reached Daniel Poole's cottage, she found Nancy already there, bent over his body with a stethoscope.

Nell Stillwell hovered nearby. Nell, who, along with her husband, Horace, ran the butcher shop, was one of the town's main sources of news and gossip. She seemed always to know everything that was happening, and just to make certain she didn't miss anything, she made it a habit to stop by the surgery often to find out whether Nancy had learned some tidbit she didn't already know herself. At first she created imaginary ailments on her part to provide an excuse for her surgery visits, but when she ran out of maladies, she continued to stop by anyway. She apparently felt she no longer needed an excuse to gather or dispense information.

"No sign of blood, no sign of anything. Died just like the others," Nell said by way of greeting when she saw Alexandra. "No sign of blood on his body anyway. Just that spot on his apron. Why was he wearing that thing anyway?"

Nancy glanced up from her examination and nodded her agreement with Nell's observation.

"What's happening to our men?" Nell asked. "They's dying like flies. Some claim that ghost knight is really Snow hisself. Not right for him to abandon us like that. Not right for him to kill people, either."

"We've no proof that anyone killed anyone," Alexandra said, "and certainly not that Constable Snow committed such a crime." Alexandra pulled her stethoscope from her medical bag. "What do you think, Nancy?"

"No sign of trauma. Looks like an apoplexy. Except he's so young. Of course, youth doesn't always protect a person from diseases of the heart, but—"

"That smell!" Alexandra said, interrupting Nancy. "Did you notice it?"

"I smelt it," Nell said. "Vomited, he did. Seen it on the ground. Fear makes a person do that. Somebody scared the vomit out of 'im."

"I saw the bile," Nancy said, "but now that you mention it, yes, there's something else." She bent over the corpse and sniffed. "Smells good. Rather like, I don't know, something sweet."

"It's the same scent I detected on the horseman," Alexandra said.

"Horseman?" Nell asked, forcing her way toward the body. "You mean the ghost knight? You seen 'im?" She sniffed. "I see what you mean by that smell. Smells like cakes baking, don't it? You smelled it before? On the ghost knight? Danny Poole was the ghost knight?"

"We must get Mr. Poole's body to Percy Gibbs," Alexandra said, ignoring Nell's barrage of questions.

Nancy looked at Alexandra and seemed to read her mind. "You're going to. . . ." She stopped speaking and glanced at Nell with a guilty look, then back at Alexandra.

Alexandra gave Nancy a cautionary look before she spoke to Nell. "Please ask Mr. Stillwell if we can borrow his wagon to transport the body. Oh, and see if you can find another able-bodied man to help your husband. It's never easy to lift a lifeless body."

"I'll fetch the men and the meat wagon right away," Nell said, hurrying away toward the butcher shop.

"You're thinking of doing an autopsy," Nancy said in a low voice when Nell was out of hearing range.

"I'm not allowed to do autopsies, you know that," Alexandra said. "That's a task reserved for male physicians."

"You're thinking of doing an autopsy," Nancy repeated.

"You must think you're quite clever to presume to know my thoughts."

"Ha!" Nancy said. "'Tis not that hard when I've been with you as long as I have. And it won't be the first time you've broken that particular law, now will it? Are you going to ask Lord Dunsford to help you again?"

"If I remember correctly, the last time Lord Dunsford observed an autopsy he developed problems with his digestion and had to leave the building."

"I'll get the boys to keep watch for us outside the mortuary while we do it," Nancy said.

"I have never said I am going to perform an autopsy, and I certainly never said *we* would perform one. I couldn't be responsible for enticing you to break the law even if I did so myself, but, of course, I have no plans for such a thing."

"Don't worry about getting in after the building is closed," Nancy said as if Alexandra had not just offered an elaborate protest. "Rob can manage that for us, just like he did the last time. And if my memory serves me, you had no problem with me being there when you broke the law before."

Chapter 9

Alexandra and Nancy accompanied Deputy Poole's body, secured away in the meat wagon, to the undertaker's house. Percy Gibbs greeted them with one of his scriptural proclamations. "Through envy of the devil came death into the world."

"You can't fool us, Percy," Nancy retorted. "You don't believe in the devil."

"Nor in God either," Percy said as he set about unloading the body with the help of one of his workers.

"Will you be wanting to examine the body?" Percy asked.

"Yes," Alexandra said without looking at him. "But I'm afraid I don't have the time at the moment. I shall do the exam later." She knew he was referring to a cursory examination of the body and not an autopsy.

"I know I don't have to tell you that you mustn't wait too long. You know the way of all flesh as well as I know it myself." Percy stood back from the wagon now as his workers pushed the gurney on which the body had been placed. His hands were folded in front of him in what might have been called a pious manner if it had been anyone else.

"I shall get to the task as soon as possible," Alexandra said.

"And I shall do all I can to help," Percy said. "Now that I shan't be bothered with repairing locks. Did I mention that someone broke the lock on the door sometime back?"

"Oh, what a shame," Alexandra said. She felt certain he was referring to the lock Rob had broken for her the last time she'd found it necessary to perform an illegal autopsy.

"Rather an expensive repair. And surprising. It's hard to imagine why anyone would want to break into a place where there's nothing save dead bodies and coffins."

"Indeed," Alexandra said, feeling more and more uncomfortable with the conversation.

"I don't want any more broken locks. I prefer going about my work with the dead to trying to repair the contraptions. Should have called the locksmith. `Twould have saved time, not to mention money, since I broke a lock trying to install it. But, that, of course, is my own concern and none of yours. As I said, I am eager to be of any help I can." His eyes bore into Alexandra's gaze.

Alexandra looked at him in silence for a moment. "I appreciate your offer," she said, finally. Was he offering to leave the building unlocked so she could accomplish her clandestine deed without doing the damage she had done before when Rob broke the lock for her?

"It seems as if we're completely without law enforcement in Newton-upon-Sea with the constable gone and the deputy dead. Could offer opportunities for those who wish to break the law," Percy continued. "I should think if one were inclined, one wouldn't even have to wait until darkness falls."

"Quite so," Alexandra said. "Now, if you'll excuse me, I must get back to my medical practice."

When they were safely out the door, Nancy leaned toward Alexandra and whispered, "Now there was an invitation if ever I heard one."

Alexandra didn't reply. Why bother when she knew Nancy was already reading her mind?

"I think it best we wait until darkness falls, nevertheless," Nancy added. "Wouldn't want any passersby to see us."

"You're quite wise, Nancy," Alexandra said without looking at her. "Now, we won't speak of this again until the time comes."

The time came sooner than either Nancy or Alexandra expected. They were able to close the surgery earlier than usual, and Alexandra called Artie and Rob into the house to give them instructions.

"Zack almost gave us away last time," Alexandra said, speaking to both of them. "Your job is to keep Zack quiet while all three of you keep watch for anyone who might happen by. Zack has acted as a watch dog for me before, but he's not always discreet. You must do your best to keep him quiet so he won't attract attention."

"We'll be going to the house of the dead again?" Artie asked. "Like we done that time before. That time ye cut into that bloke's body and looked at his innards?"

"Yes," Nancy said, answering for Alexandra. "That's exactly what we'll be doing."

Arties shuddered. "All I can say is, ye's got more guts than most."

"Mind yer mouth, Artie!" Rob scolded. "Ye's not to use such language with ladies."

"What? Ye means guts? She's a doctor, ain't she? She knows what guts is."

"I said mind yer mouth!" This time Rob accompanied his words with a scuff at Artie's head.

"Enough from the two of you!" Nancy warned. "Now get your caps and a leash for Zack and go on ahead of us. You're to make it look as if you're out for a stroll with the dog."

"Then the two of ye will come up and break into the place." Rob was unable to keep the excitement out of his voice. "I swears, if the two of ye hadn't chose the healing professions, ye coulda been thieves and scoundrels with the best of us. Never meant that in a bad way," he added quickly when he saw the frown on Nancy's face and her mouth open as if she was about to scold again.

"We can all do without your opinion of what Dr. Gladstone and I are suited for," Nancy said. "Now, keep your mouths shut and do your job."

Alexandra and Nancy gave the boys a few minutes to get ahead of them before they started out on foot back to the village. Alexandra didn't want to risk riding Lucy and leaving her tied anywhere near the mortuary in case someone remembered seeing the little mare who was familiar to everyone in Newton-upon-Sea.

As they approached the building where the mortuary was housed, Alexandra felt a sudden void in her chest when she saw Percy. He was on foot with his wife on his arm. All he did, however, was touch the brim of his hat as he met the two of them, and Mrs. Gibbs gave them a smile of greeting before they continued on their way. Alexandra was almost certain, however, that Percy had winked as he passed by. That was quite a different reaction than he'd had before when she'd found it necessary to perform a post mortem examination. At that time, both he and Constable Snow had been unwilling to give permission for the task, not only because she was female, but because they'd insisted on her providing written permission from the family, something that, at the time, was impossible. This time, since no law officer was available, the question hadn't arisen. Alexandra knew she was taking a risk, nevertheless.

They were within a few feet of the entrance when both of them noticed Rob and Artie across the street and several yards beyond. Tossing a stick for Zack, they pretended not to see Nancy and Alexandra and quickly distracted Zack when he seemed about to bound across the street to greet his mistress. Rob pulled something soft and dripping blood from a bag and held it under the dog's nose for him to gobble. That would have given Nancy and Alexandra just enough time to disappear around the back of the mortuary building had not Nicholas ridden by on his fine Arabian horse.

"Good evening, ladies. I hope it's not a medical emergency that brings you out this evening." He was eyeing Alexandra's medical bag.

" No, my lord," Alexandra said, her voice strained.

"I saw the boys across the street and wondered—"

"You *could* say it was an emergency of sorts," Nancy said. "So I think it best we move along, don't you, miss?"

"Well if you need. . . ." Nicholas stopped speaking and seemed to take sudden notice of where they were. "Oh, I see," he said. "That again. You must allow me to help."

"You were more of a hindrance than a help in a similar situation in the past." Alexandra kept her voice low, and there was a hint of anxiety in her tone. She wanted him to move on.

"If I know the law regarding these things, then I'm certain you are breaking—"

"I have no doubt that you know the law, my lord," Alexandra said.

"Quite so," Nicholas said. "And since that is the case, you must call upon me immediately should you suffer any consequences."

"Thank you, my lord." The conversation was making Alexandra even more nervous, and after her curt response, she moved away from Nicholas with quick steps. She, along with Nancy, went to the back of the building. To her surprise, Nicholas had dismounted his horse and was following closely behind. She opened the door with slow caution, grateful to find it unlocked. She stepped inside, followed by Nancy and then Nicholas. There was little light in the room, and it was cold, somewhat like the interior of a cave. The smell of decay was unmistakable, along with a caustic chemical smell.

"My lord Dunsford," Alexandra said. "I'm afraid you will find this as unpleasant as you did before when you tried to witness the same procedure. I suggest you retire to Montmarsh, and I shall inform you of any pertinent results later."

"Why do you always revert to calling me *my lord* when you're nervous? I'm still Nicholas, and I have no intention of telling anyone of your crime. And you needn't worry about me. I'm sure I'll be quite all right."

Alexandra took a deep breath and tried to refrain from rolling her eyes. "Very well," she said and walked toward the interior of the large, cavernous room where a body lay on a table, covered with a sheet. By this time, Nancy had lit two oil lamps and set them up next to the white lump that was the body.

Alexandra lifted the sheet to reveal a face. Although still recognizable, it had grown paler and more waxen looking than it had been the last time she'd seen it. She couldn't help remembering Danny Poole as a young boy, several years her junior, rough-housing with other boys in the streets of Newton-upon-Sea or running along the coast line, his hair tousled by the breeze. She touched the deputy's chest and noted the coolness, yet there was still a small amount of blanching of the skin under her fingertips. It would be a few more hours before full rigor mortis was established.

Working silently beside Alexandra, Nancy opened the medical bag and began to lay out instruments on a table next to where the body rested. Before Alexandra picked up a scalpel, she opened the mouth for examination. She found two teeth in the process of decay and a raw wound on the gums near one of the bad teeth. She'd seen the problem in others. Gums often became diseased in the presence of bad teeth. Such a sore could provide an opening for microscopic, disease-causing organisms, or even poison, to enter the blood and attack various organs. Once she was back in her surgery, she would examine all of the organs available to her. She also snipped a sample of hair from the dead man's head.

She made the first incision across the chest from shoulder to shoulder, and then another incision along the abdomen all the way to the pubis. She was vaguely aware of Nicholas standing behind her, but he made no sound or any apparent movements. She removed the liver first and placed it in a pan provided by Nancy. She would dissect the organ later and examine pieces under a microscope. Next, she removed the adrenal glands and kidneys, then the stomach, pancreas, and intestines, examining each carefully as they were removed. When she opened the stomach to examine the contents, she thought she detected the faintly sweet scent she'd noted in the presence of the horseman. There was no way to be certain, however, since she often found her sense of smell distorted during such procedures.

Alexandra and Nancy worked for several hours before Alexandra signaled that it was time to close the incision and leave with the samples of organs Nancy had incised from each of them. Alexandra would have preferred to have access to each entire organ, but transporting them to her surgery would have been difficult if not impossible.

"Nicholas! You're still here," she said as she turned around, holding her blood-stained hands in front of her on the way to wash them at the pump and basin at the end of the room.

"Yes," he said. "I have to admit it wasn't easy to stay. Nevertheless, I found it fascinating, and your skills amazing. You will take those little bits of the body you harvested to your microscope for examination, I assume."

Alexandra nodded and wiped her forehead awkwardly with her upper arm where her sleeve was not bloodied.

"You look exhausted. You as well as Nancy."

"It's hard work," she said, almost too tired to speak.

"I shall see that you get home safely," Nicholas said. "If only I'd known I was going to do this, I would have brought my carriage."

At that moment, the sound of Zack's loud and angry bark reverberated through the room. Nancy and Alexandra looked at each other, alarmed.

"Someone's out there," Nancy whispered.

Alexandra nodded and finished washing her hands under the pump.

"No one knows we're here, do they?" Nicholas asked.

"We can't be sure," Nancy said, still whispering as she pumped water for her own washing.

Zack barked again, even louder, and the three of them inside the mortuary could hear the shouts of the two boys. It was not possible to make out what they were saying, except for the word *no,* repeated several times. There was a loud clatter at the front door as if someone was trying to enter, and then the sound of several voices. The three of them ran to front and saw the door shaking on its hinges as something banged against it.

From the front window, they could see a mob, of about twenty-five men, along with a few women. Their faces were distorted by the light from the torches they held high above them. It was a milling, rumbling, boiling pot of rage.

"They know we're in here!" Nancy said. "They want to kill us!"

"Of course they don't want to kill us," Alexandra said. "That would be rather extreme." Her words belied her feelings. Her heart was about to leap out of her chest, and all that was in her screamed for her escape, but she knew if she tried, she would be detected. She made herself walk into the parlor and closer to the undulating front door. If anyone out there was in danger, she had to be ready.

"I seen her go in there, and I know what she's doing!" a male voice shouted.

"Ye's wrong, sir, the lady doctor ain't in there!" This was Rob's voice, as loud as that of the man he was confronting.

"She's in there all right! That beast of dog, he's always where she is," another man yelled. "See 'im? `E's out here waitin' for her."

"Stop hittin' that door. Ye's sure to break it if you don't stop!" Artie's little-boy voice could barely be heard above the sound of the other shouts and the hammering on the door.

There was more pounding, more shouts from the mob.

"They've got Rob!" Nancy screamed and backed away from the window.

Alexandra lunged for the door but backed away when she saw a chip of wood fall from the facing where the hinge was attached.

"Stay here, both of you!" Nicholas said, striding toward the back door. "Stay away from that door."

Alexandra started to protest, but Nicholas had already disappeared into the embalming room, headed for the back exit.

"What can we do?" Nancy's voice was strained.

Before Alexandra could reply, the door bulged inward as another loud and forceful blow came from the outside Nancy screamed, and Alexandra reached for her to pull her close. "We have to stay calm," she said. She felt anything but calm. She was torn between staying inside as Nicholas had commanded and trying to rescue Rob.

She made her way to the window and saw Rob struggling to free himself from the grip of two men. They'd forced his arms behind his back, and she could hear his cries of pain. Nicholas appeared suddenly, emerging from the back of the building.

"Stop ! Stop in the name of the queen's court!" Nicholas shouted.

"'Tis his lordship," one of the men cried. "'Tis the earl hisself!"

"In the name of the queen's court," Nicholas shouted again, his voice sharp and commanding.

The mob grew quieter, but Alexandra could see them still seething and stirring, still ready to pounce.

"You!" Nicholas pointed to a man in front of him. "What's this is all about?"

Alexandra saw, in the dancing light of the torches, Rob using the momentary distraction to jerk himself free. He ran toward Zack and Artie at the edge of the crowd. One of the men started after him, but he was stopped by another who pointed toward Nicholas, urging him to listen. Artie held on to Zack's leash as the massive dog lunged toward the crowd. Rob reached them just in time to help Artie hold the dog back from the mob.

"Zack! No!" Again it was Nicholas' voice shouting a command, and, to Alexandra's surprise, Zack obeyed. He stopped barking and lunging, although he stood alert and tense.

"Talk!" Nicholas said, pointing to the man he had earlier commanded to speak. "Why are you trying to tear down this building?"

"She's in there!" the man said. "She's in there performing an ungodly deed on a dead man!"

"Who are you accusing?" Nicholas asked.

"Gladstone! That woman what calls herself a doctor! Gladstone!" The men kept shouting, each trying to be louder than the others.

"You're accusing Dr. Gladstone of an ungodly deed?" Nicholas asked. "Explain that to me. What ungodly deed?"

"Why, she cuts the body open and slices it piece by piece!" one of the men said.

"Goes against the will of God!" the other said. "'Tis only Frenchmen and the like that defiles a body that way."

"Why would Dr. Gladstone do such a thing?" Nicholas asked in a much calmer voice.

"God knows why," came the answer.

"'Tis called a necropsy," the other voice said. "I heard of it before. Has a Latin, popeish sound to it, I say."

"A necropsy, yes, I've heard of that," Nicholas said. "Sometimes called an autopsy. I believe there are distinguished doctors in London who perform them."

"Even if they does, it ain't right for a woman to do a man like that."

"I say, I never thought of that," Nicholas said. "I'd say that calls for a good discussion. What do you say we talk about it over a pitcher of ale at the Blue Ram?"

"Ale you say? A whole pitcher?" It was impossible for Alexandra to determine which of the men was speaking, since Nicholas had persuaded them to speak in quieter voices.

"I'm buying, of course." There was no mistaking Nicholas' voice.

"Never turned down a pitcher o' ale," one of them said. There were a few more fading and incomprehensible exchanges as the men moved away toward the Blue Ram.

Chapter 10

Nancy and Alexandra were in the kitchen sharing a breakfast of poached eggs and toast with Rob and Artie. Alexandra often allowed the boys to eat with them when the weather was exceptionally cold or stormy. This morning, though the weather was pleasant, she'd insisted that Nancy invite them in as a reward for their service the night before.

"I can't imagine how we could have gotten through the night without you," Alexandra said. "Had it not been for the two of you and Lord Dunsford, I fear we'd be in a great deal of trouble."

Rob shrugged. "Had to do somethin', now didn't we? What with the constable gone and now 'e's deputy dead and whittled up by the two of you."

"We don't *whittle* a body when we perform an autopsy," Nancy said, "and the doctor is correct. Even with law enforcement unavailable, we could have been lynched by a mob. Stop slurping your tea, Artie."

"Like you say, Lord Dunsford done his part same as me and Artie and old Zack," Rob said.

"Yes," Alexandra agreed. "You were all brave."

"Surprised, I was," Nancy said.

"We were all surprised at what happened," Alexandra said.

"What I mean is, I was surprised by Lord Dunsford. The way he took on that mob. Didn't know he had it in him. I think Zack was impressed as well." Nancy dabbed at a spot on the table where Artie had spilled his tea.

Alexandra looked at her with raised eyebrows. "What an odd thing for you to say, Nancy. One could almost say you see Lord Dunsford as a coward."

"Not a coward exactly, miss, but he is a bit of dandy, you know. Not the type to take on the likes of men about to start a street brawl. I take it you weren't surprised."

"Not at all," Alexandra said. "No more than I was surprised at the bravery of the boys and Zack."

Artie smiled broadly, and Rob ducked his head, embarrassed, but Alexandra could see a self-satisfied grin on his face.

"Just because we were lucky enough to escape with our lives last night doesn't mean our trouble is over," Nancy said.

Alexandra's sigh sounded troubled. "I'm well aware of that, Nancy. Since we weren't able to talk to Lord Dunsford, we don't know where we stand with the mob."

"Or the law, for that matter." Nancy spoke with her back to Alexandra and the others as she stood at the stove, serving up more eggs for the two boys.

"We is back runnin' from the coppers?" Artie asked, directing his question to Rob. The two boys had become more than familiar with trying to stay a step ahead of authorities before Alexandra and Nancy rescued them from the wharves and put them to work.

"Nothin to worry about." The break in Rob's sixteen-year-old changing voice tarnished his attempt at sounding confident. The room was silent for several seconds except for the sound of forks against plates and Artie's slurping. "Can't say I understands it all," Rob said, breaking the silence as he looked at Alexandra. "Why was them blokes so mad about what you was doin'? 'Twas just doctor work ye was doin' in there, way I sees it. Was ye up to somethin' I don't know 'bout? Breakin' the law, I mean?"

"No one was breaking laws. Shame on you for suggesting Dr. Gladstone would do such a thing," Nancy scolded. " Now, eat your eggs."

"Actually, I was breaking the law," Alexandra said, "but in this case I felt I had no choice."

"I knows what ye means by that," Rob said, speaking around the mouthful of eggs he was chewing. "Many's the time I stole a few pence or maybe a slab o' bacon. Had no other choice since it was that or starve to death. Not to mention what woulda become of Artie. He'd starve in no time at all, him bein' such a skinny runt. So ye done it because we's all about to starve, did ye? If the problem is that people ain't payin' ye on time, I can speed 'em up. I has me ways."

"For heaven's sake, Rob--" Nancy began.

"It's nothing like that," Alexandra said, interrupting her. "I was breaking the law by performing the autopsy on Deputy Poole."

"Oh yeah," Rob said. "Ye was whittlin' on the poor bloke's body so ye could come up with what kilt 'im. Ain't the first time ye had to sneak around to get it done."

"It's illegal for a woman to perform an autopsy, for one thing," Alexandra said, "and I didn't have the proper permission."

"Well, it ain't always convenient to wait for permission. I learned that back when I was even littler than Artie. But as for ye bein' a woman, I sees the point, ye bein' the weaker sex, as they says."

"Weaker sex?" Nancy's screech was indignant. "I'll tell you about weaker—"

She was interrupted by the sound of someone knocking on a door and Zack's single bark, signaling a visitor. Alexandra and Nancy exchanged a silent glance, fearing they were both about to have to answer for what they'd done the night before.

"I'll see who it is," Nancy said, hurrying toward the front. "You stay here, and I'll tell whoever it is you're with a patient."

"No, Nancy," Alexandra said. "I'll go to the door. I'm the one who should handle this." She was well aware of all of them, Nancy, Zack, and the boys, following her as she made her way to the front door and opened it to Nicholas.

"Lord Dunsford!" she said, using his formal title because of the presence of her entourage.

"At your service, doctor," Nicholas said with mock formality.

"Come in, please. I'm so eager to talk to you."

"I'm sure you are," he said, keeping an eye on Zack as he entered. Zack, however, did not make the customary growl when he saw Nicholas. Instead, he stood still and tense, his ears pointed upward as he had done the night before when Nicholas confronted the mob.

"Tea for Lord Dunsford, Nancy," Alexandra said. "Finish your breakfast and then back to work," she added, turning to Artie and Rob.

Alexandra led him toward the parlor. "Now, tell me what happened last night and whether or not I'm going to need the services of a good London barrister." Her flippant remark belied the terrible anxiety she felt.

"Of course you need a good London barrister," he said. "Doesn't everyone?" he added when he saw the look she gave him. "And as for what happened last night, all I can say is that I believe I managed to turn down the flame under a pot that was about to boil over. Can't say how long that will last."

"How did you do it? How did you keep them from coming back and lynching me?"

"Oh, I simply used an old and reliable technique. I lied."

"You--?"

"I told them that you were no longer in the coroner's building, although I assured them that they did see you go inside in all likelihood, but that you went in on the instructions of Constable Snow to make certain all was in order with the body."

"But they know Constable Snow is not here."

"Certainly they do. I told him that you had received a telegraph message from him, instructing you as to what you must do."

"And they believed you?"

"I showed them the telegram."

"How could you have possibly done that? I've received no such telegram, and you know that. You also know that no one knows how to reach Constable Snow to apprise him of what's going on in Newton-upon-Sea."

"All right, let's just say I showed him *a* telegram. I happened to have one in my pocket I'd received it earlier from my office advising me of the postponement of a court date."

"But if it wasn't from the constable advising me—"

"I was counting on them not being able to read, and it worked. What I showed them looked like a telegram, and they accepted that I knew what it said."

"The fire under that boiling pot could very easily flare up again," Alexandra said, just as Nancy entered with the tea.

"Then I suppose I'll have do some more quick thinking," Nicholas said. In spite of his flippant remark, his brow was creased with a worried frown. He stayed long enough to finish his tea before he left to allow Alexandra to make her morning rounds to see patients.

Alexandra went to Olive Fontaine's house first, out of concern for her being elderly and living alone. Mrs. Fontaine opened her door and welcomed Alexandra with her usual graciousness while her four cats curled around her ankles. Zack was, as always, leery of the alien creatures and barked when he saw them. By now, he had come to anticipate Alexandra's command to stay quiet and not start a chase. It was clear by the look in his eyes that he did not obey the command with any enthusiasm and instead wanted with all that was in him to follow his natural instincts. A raised back and a hiss from the yellow cat gave him second thoughts, and he took a step backward. Mrs. Fontaine quickly closed the door, leaving Zack outside, before the drama could come to a climax.

"You're such a dear to stop by so often to make sure of my well-being," she said. "Your father would have been so proud of you. I'm sure you know that without my telling you. Huntington always spoke of you in glowing terms. Always mentioned how, had you not been born female, you could have become one of the kingdom's stellar physicians."

Her remarks caused a mixture of embarrassment and chagrin in Alexandra. "How nice of you to mention it," she finally managed to say. "Now, tell me how you're feeling."

"Quite well, as always," Mrs. Fontaine said. "From a physical standpoint, at least, although I must confess anguish over the recent events in Newton."

"Who can blame you? We all feel distress."

"I was about to have a cup of tea," Mrs. Fontaine said. "Will you join me? Nothing like tea shared with a friend to cheer one up. Especially when there are scones spread with honey."

"Thank you, I've had more than enough tea this morning, but I can't resist a scone with honey."

"I'll be back with it soon. Brush the cats away if they bother you," Mrs. Fontaine said over her shoulder as she disappeared into the kitchen. She reemerged with a tray holding a teapot and cup, plates of scones, and a small bowl of honey. "I wish you'd been here just a bit earlier. Young Judith was just here. We could have all had tea together. Such a lovely girl."

"She is indeed," Alexandra said as she accepted a plate.

"She's the image of her mother."

"Judith told me her family came from Foulness," Alexandra said. "How is it that you know her mother?"

"The Payne family is one of the oldest families in England, my dear, and besides, we're distantly related. I was a Payne before I married. Judith's branch of the family settled in Foulness, while my family came to Newton-upon-Sea, as did the Fontaines, another old line family."

"Then you must know Judith's father, George Payne."

"Oh yes, of course, and his parents as well. As a matter of fact, I was present when little George was born. God rest his mother's soul. She would have been proud of him."

"Indeed?"

"Oh yes. Followed in his own father's footsteps and rose in the ranks of the brotherhood to become Grand Master of the Freemasons. A shame he was not as successful in business as his father was. The Paynes were merchant bankers, you know. Started out as salt merchants, of course, but moved on to other things, as did all our old line families. I'm afraid young George was a bit of a dreamer and never quite fit into the banking business. Still, he's a fine man at heart."

"I see."

Mrs. Fontaine scrutinized Alexandra's face. "What is it you're not saying? Do I detect doubt? Suspicion?"

"Well, you see it's just that. . . ."

"Go on," Mrs. Fontaine urged.

"I don't want to sound like a gossip, but I've heard Judith didn't get on well with her father."

"Oh that!" Mrs. Fontaine said with a wave of her hand while she used her other hand to lift one of her cats from where it had found a comfortable nest on the top of her head. "That really is nothing more than gossip—a silly rumor started by a cousin in Foulness. Men can be such gossips, although it's always women who get the blame, isn't it?"

"I suppose that's true."

"Of course, it's true. In this case, it was a cousin who was jealous of George's advancement in the brotherhood."

"Grand Master, you mentioned."

"Oh yes. Quite an honor, I understand. Master over several lodges in the area. You know how those Freemasons are. Ah, of course you don't know. Huntington never got around to joining, even though he was invited several times. I know because my own husband told me. Always too busy, I suppose. Nevertheless, those who do find the time take their positions and their power quite seriously, so it's understandable, even if it's not excusable, that a jealous cousin might try to do something underhanded to discredit his more successful relative. Now, I see that look on your face, and I quite agree. It's all so petty and childish, but some boys never grow up, you know."

"You don't believe the rumor then, that Judith and her father are—well at least at odds if not estranged."

"Of course not. Mind you, I'm not saying they didn't have their disagreements. Judith has more than a few modern notions that rub her father the wrong way. "Always going on about that woman, Mary Something, who wrote that book about women and their rights."

"Mary Wollstonecraft. She wrote *A Vindication of the Rights of Woman.*"

"Yes, that's it. Never read it myself. Have you?"

"I have. It's quite an old book. Written almost a hundred years ago."

"My education is lacking, I suppose. Judith tells me that's the premise of Mrs. Wollstonecraft's work—that women aren't inferior to men, but only appear to be because they're denied an equal education."

"A reasonable summary, I'd say. She believed that if reason could prevail, women would have all of the opportunities of men."

"Oh yes. That kind of talk infuriated her father. They could argue for hours about such things."

"Do you believe George Payne could be guilty of something that is, shall we say, sinister?"

Mrs. Fontaine frowned. "I don't know what you're getting at. George Payne is the last person in the world you would call sinister. He's a fine man. I should like to introduce you to him sometime. You'll find him every bit as agreeable as Judith."

"I'm sure I would, Mrs. Fontaine. Forgive me for suggesting otherwise. I'm afraid I may have been influenced by those scurrilous rumors you mentioned." She didn't want to upset Mrs. Fontaine by revealing what Judith had told her about her father.

"Understandable, I suppose, at least to some extent, but I caution you not to be taken in too easily." She was silent for a moment, looking at Alexandra. "You look so troubled. This must be quite difficult for you."

"It is, of course," Alexandra said. "As I said, it's difficult for all of us."

"But more so for you. Most of the townspeople look up to you, you know. You're one of our problem solvers. Now with Robert, excuse me, Constable Snow gone and young Daniel dead, much falls on your shoulders."

"It's true," Alexandra said with a sigh. "I do wish Constable Snow would return. If ever we needed him, it's now."

"I quite agree." Mrs. Fontaine had a concerned look on her face, as if it were she who had taken the town's burdens on her own shoulders.

"Try not to worry, Mrs. Fontaine. "Lord Dunsford has sought the help of Scotland Yard to find the constable."

"Oh dear!" Mrs. Fontaine said, as if the idea of Scotland Yard becoming involved alarmed her.

"So far, Lord Dunsford hasn't received a response," Alexandra said. "Perhaps they deem it unimportant compared to all the crime they're dealing with in London. The next step would be to ask a magistrate to appoint someone to stand in for the constable until we locate him."

"But if. . . . Oh, I see you reaching for your bag. You don't have to leave so soon, do you?"

"I'd like to stay longer. There must be a great deal more you can tell me, but we'll have to make it a later time. I'm afraid I have too many patients to see today." Alexandra didn't tell her that she also needed time to collect her thoughts. She needed to know if Judith had been lying to her about her father, or if it were Mrs. Fontaine who was lying. Or it could be that Mrs. Fontaine was simply confused. Confusion was not uncommon in the elderly, although Olive Fontaine had not shown signs of declining mental capacity. She seemed as fit as anyone twenty years her junior might be.

Alexandra tried to put the troublesome question to the back of her mind as she made her morning rounds. Her last patient was Charlotte Malcolm and her new son, both of whom were still in precarious health.

By the time she left the young mother and her baby, there was little time left before surgery hours would start, but she wanted to stop by Judith's cottage, there was much to ask her. When Alexandra got to the house, however, no one answered the door. Zack wandered off and proceeded to dig a hole in the soft garden soil where Judith had just planted flowers.

Alexandra scolded him and called him to her side. He obeyed and sat at her feet. Once again Alexandra knocked and called Judith's name, but there was still no answer. She was about to leave when a woman in the next house over stepped out of her door.

"Looking for Miss Payne, are you, Dr. Gladstone? Well, you won't find 'er. Gone to Foulness, she has."

"Zack!" Alexandra called, scolding him again, this time because he had hiked his leg against a beautiful, tall flowering plant.

"Left early this morning," the woman said, although Alexandra was having a difficult time listening to her since Zack insisted on being so distracting. "Said she got a message from some bloke what came down from Foulness. A terrible tragedy. Yer dog is diggin', e' is. Get away, dog!" She turned back to Alexandra. "Left me in charge of the garden. Don't know how long she'll be gone. Her father kilt himself. Poor Miss Payne. May take 'er some time to get everything settled, don't you know."

Chapter 11

"I suppose it's not so very long, but am I the only one who has noticed that ever since Daniel Poole died, there has been not another mysterious death in the parish?" Nancy asked a nearly a week later. She was removing human tissue from a bottle of formaldehyde for Alexandra to examine under the microscope. They were both frustrated that so far, they had found nothing to confirm their suspicion of poisoning.

"If you're saying Deputy Poole killed the others, it makes even less sense than blaming Constable Snow. After all, Deputy Poole is one of the victims," Alexandra said as she took her seat in front of the microscope to examine the tissue.

"He could have died of another cause."

"And there's the strange occurrence of the bloody apron. . . ."

Nancy sighed. "I suppose I'm just trying to invent ways not to make the constable look guilty."

"Finding the cause of Daniel Poole's death might help," Alexandra said. "I only wish I could find that cause. There is something odd in the liver tissue, but I can't determine what." Alexandra continued to study the specimen carefully and write notes on a pad next to the microscope as she worked.

After a few minutes, Nancy demanded her attention again. "Think about this: No one has seen the horseman since Daniel Poole's death."

"Couldn't we say the same thing about Judith Payne?" Alexandra asked. "She's been gone several days as well."

"She's been back almost two days."

"Oh, then I must stop by and see her," Alexandra said. She wasn't particularly surprised that Nancy knew about Judith's return. She was privy to most of the town's gossip, usually by patients who stopped by the surgery while Alexandra was making her rounds.

"Nell Stillwell told me," Nancy said, as if to confirm Alexandra's thoughts.

"Nell's not ill, I hope."

"Of course not. You know Nell."

"Yes, I do indeed." Alexandra knew that Nell often stopped by the surgery while Alexandra was on her rounds to make sure Nancy hadn't heard some tidbit of gossip she herself hadn't heard at the butcher shop. Ever since the Newton Press had stopped printing its weekly broadsheet a few years earlier, Nell had served as the main conveyer of news. It didn't seem to bother most villagers that her reports weren't always accurate.

"Poor girl's terribly upset, as one might imagine. Nell said Mrs. Fontaine has had Judith staying at her house. She believes Judith shouldn't be alone. Staying with Mrs. Fontaine and those cats. Can you imagine?"

"I haven't seen Mrs. Fontaine since late last week," Alexandra said, "much to my embarrassment. I try to see her at least every two days, but I'm afraid I've let myself become distracted with the specimens I've been studying. Nevertheless, even if I saw everyone in town daily, I doubt I could keep up to date on the gossip as well as you, Nancy."

"'Tisn't necessarily gossip." Nancy sounded defensive. 'Tis usually things you need to know."

"I'm sure you're right," Alexandra said as she slid her microscope back. The first patient was sure to arrive soon.

A frantic Charlotte Malcolm arrived with her baby, still only a few weeks old. They were brought in by an even more frantic Samuel, who carried the baby cradled in one arm while Charlotte leaned heavily on the other arm.

"He's turned bilious!" Charlotte cried in a feeble voice that was barely audible. She was still weak from her surgery, and as white as her baby was yellow. "He's dying!" she cried. "See how he's turning color. Like a dead person, he is. He's already part dead!"

"You shouldn't be out of bed," Alexandra said, leading her to a chair. "And your baby is not dying. He's jaundiced."

"He's what?" Samuel asked, looking every bit as frightened as his young wife.

"Plenty of babies get it," Nancy said in an attempt to calm both of them. "Sometimes 'tis called Yellow Gum. Perhaps you've heard of that."

Samuel shook his head, eyes wide with fright.

"Yellow Gum! Babies die of yellow gum," Charlotte said as Nancy led her to an examination table and put a stethoscope to her chest.

"Your baby is not going to die," Alexandra said. "I'll give him a compound of rhubarb and potassia. He also needs sunshine. Now that the weather is warmer, you must take him outdoors wearing only his nappie so he can soak up as much sun as possible."

"She can't do it," Samuel said. "She's too weak to carry 'im."

"Then you must do it for her," Alexandra said. "Every day for at least an hour." She turned to Charlotte. "Are you able to nurse the child?"

"Can't you see she can't do nothin'!" Samuel cried before his wife could answer. "She's dyin' same as the babe. Heart beats so fast it makes 'er faint."

Nancy, with the stethoscope still in place, removed it and gave Alexandra a nod. "Palpitations," she said. Before Alexandra could respond, Nancy had already turned around and reached for a compound of iron and quinine.

"Take the compound Nancy is getting for you three times a day," Alexandra said. "You must eat more beef and mutton. Eat it every day. I'll have Nell Stillwell deliver it to you, and we'll find a wet nurse for the baby."

"Wet nurse?" Samuel said. "Beef and mutton? How am I to pay for all of it?"

"You will find a way if you want your wife and child to live," Alexandra said. She was used to helping patients work out means of payment. The wet nurse, she knew, would take payment in the form of vegetables from the garden, and Nell, at the butchers, as disagreeable as she could be at times, would provide the meat with a deep cut into her profits for a limited time at least.

As soon as surgery hours were over, Alexandra left her house for a walk to town with Zack at her side. She wanted to see Nell and Horace at the butcher shop to tell them about Charlotte's need.

"Since you're going, we could use a half pound of bacon," Nancy told her as she was leaving. Before she was more than a few steps along the lane that led to the road to the village, she heard Rob calling to her and turned to see him, along with Artie, running toward her.

"Walking to the village, are ye?" Rob asked.

"Yes," she answered, enjoying the warmth of the spring day, "I have an errand in town."

"Ain't good for ye to be goin' alone," Artie said.

"Why would you say that?" Alexandra asked. "You know that I go all over the parish alone. Except for Zack, of course."

"We best go along to protect ye," Artie said.

"If you wish." Alexandra smiled to herself at the thought of Artie, who was no more than four feet tall and weighed perhaps five stone, protecting her from anything.

"The little bugger. . . excuse me, what I mean is the boy is right, ye best not be goin' by yerself," Rob said. "Even if ye's used to doin' it in the past, things is different now, what with all them people dyin' and all them people tryin' to get at ye when ye was carvin' up that bloke. And then there's that scary chap on the horse."

Alexandra cringed at yet another description of her work, but she managed a smile nevertheless. "Very well, come along, I shall enjoy the company."

When they reached the village, the streets were quiet, since the day was winding down, and most people had gone home. When they reached the butcher shop, she could see through the front window that Nell was inside behind the counter. By this time of day, Horace would be in the back tending to the pigs and chickens they kept to butcher and sell to the public, along with the beef, mutton, fish, and oysters they relied on local farmers and fishermen to supply. The Stillwells didn't like the idea of dogs coming into the store, lest they try to gobble down the meat that was on display, so Alexandra instructed the boys to keep Zack outside, a distance from the door, so he wouldn't be tempted by the smell of a fresh raw meal.

"Well, if it ain't herself," Nell said when she saw Alexandra. She was busy sawing a beef carcass as she spoke. "Don't see you in here all that often, now do we? What with Nancy doin' the shoppin' all the time." Nell had to turn her head slightly sideways, because she had only one good eye. The other one looked egg-shell white and just as brittle--a result of failing to follow Alexandra's instructions to care for an infection a few years ago.

"You're right, of course, but Nancy did send me to purchase a half pound of bacon," Alexandra said, looking at the display of meat. None of it looked appetizing. She was not at all squeamish about the flesh and blood of a human body, but uncooked meat made her queasy.

"Bacon, of course,. I'll carve it for you now," Nell said and disappeared into the back. She returned quickly with a slab white with fat and cut into thick slices. She slapped it on the counter and pulled off a length of paper to wrap it. "Is there anything else?" she asked.

"As a matter of fact, there is," Alexandra said. "There's something I want to discuss with you. It's about Charlotte Malcolm."

"Might have known," Nell said. "Needs meat to build up 'er blood, I'd guess."

"You're right. She's quite weak."

"And just as weak in the purse, I'm sure. So you wants me to give it to 'er at a discount."

"As a matter of fact—"

"How are me and the husband supposed to live if we gives our meat away?"

"I understand your concern, but I'm not asking you to give it away."

"Just cut into me profits," Nell said, a scowl arranging itself across her face.

"Perhaps I can help," Alexandra said. "If I provide the difference between your regular price and the discount you give Charlotte and Samuel, I should think that would put your mind at ease."

Nell was silent, looking at Alexandra for several seconds. Her scowl crept deeper into the wrinkles on her face.

"In essence I would be providing your customary profit for you," Alexandra said when the pause seemed to have gone on too long.

"Ye got no business doin' that."

Alexandra looked at Nell and frowned. "I don't understand your objection. All I'll be doing is making up the difference so you can still make your customary profit."

"Ye got no business doin' that, "Nell said again. "I happens to know ye gives yer services for no charge plenty of times."

Alexandra felt nonplussed. She didn't like discussing the financial arrangements she made with her patients. "I suppose that's true, occasionally at least, but I can't afford to do it for everyone."

"Ye thinks I don't know that?" Nell sounded cross. "Don't ye see, what I'm tryin' to tell ye is ye does yer part in this village. Don't want nobody sayin' I doesn't do me own part. If I let ye do that, word would get out, mind you. I know it would. People would say we ain't charitable, me and the mister. I knows they would say such. I knows how this town gossips."

"I assure you I would keep it confidential," Alexandra told her.

Nell's laugh was derisive. "Ha! You might not say a word, but people will find out. They has their ways, and I knows all about 'em. I'll give the two youngsters their meat at a discount. Don't want nobody callin' me a pinchpenny. Don't want nobody sayin' I can't afford it either!"

"Thank you, Nell. You're quite generous. I'm sure everyone knows that," Alexandra said, feeling a mixture of self-satisfaction and guilt. She had known Nell would relent, and she'd known exactly how to bring her to it.

"If they doesn't know it, they's fools. Ye've no idea how much I gives away." Nell took a breath, as if she was afraid she'd said too much. "Now don't go spreadin' that fact around Newton-upon-Sea. Won't do to have everybody expectin' a handout."

"Certainly not," Alexandra said.

"Never know what to expect in this parish," Nell wiped her hands on her apron, leaving a greasy streak as a result of cutting off the side of bacon. The grease mingled with the blood from the beef carcass. "Everybody's gone crazy."

"I wasn't aware of that, Nell."

Nell gave her a suspicious look. "There was a mob running through town recently. Don't know what that was all about."

Alexandra was sure Nell did know, since she seemed to know everything, but she wouldn't take the bait.

"I know you must have heard of the ghost knight people sees," Nell said. "Not to mention them men dyin'. Three deaths. No coincidence if ye asks me. The Freemasons got all them secret chambers in that temple where they does them ritals as they calls 'em."

"You mean rituals."

"Whatever they's called, they's up to no good. Otherwise nothin' would be a secret. Heard they even worships a secret god. Not the Christian God, mind ye."

Alexandra started to speak, but Nell interrupted her. "I knows a bit about what goes on in this town, and I say somebody killed all three for that treasure."

"Treasure?"

"'Tis hard to believe you don't know. Been the talk around here since I was a tyke. The money in the temple of course. Buried under the floor they say."

"Oh that," Alexandra said. "Yes I've heard that story. I suppose every child in Newton-upon-Sea has heard it. It's rather like Saint Nick. Or I suppose a better example would be that it's more like that legend of a ghostly woman who rises up from the sea to snatch children who misbehave."

"Ye got it wrong, Dr. Gladstone. 'Tis no legend. 'Tis a true story. Treasure is there, but nobody will ever find it. Them old Templar Knights put a curse on it, and them Freemasons is bound by the curse."

"Perhaps I remember hearing that."

"But ye don't believe it, does ye? I can tell ye don't by that look on yer face. Just as well ye don't believe, though. Look where it got the three blokes what did believe it." She shoved the wrapped bacon toward Alexandra. "Tell Nancy I give her the best I have."

"I'll do that, Nell. Thank you. Not just for the best of your bacon, but for what you're doing for the Malcolms. And don't worry. I don't think it will take long to get Charlotte back to normal."

"And about that night of the mob. Did you learn anything when you. . . .well, you know."

"Good day, Nell."

Nell's only response as she went back to sawing at the carcass was a *humpff* that could have meant any number of things.

Chapter 12

When Alexandra arrived at Mrs. Fontaine's cottage during her morning rounds the next day, the elderly woman was in her garden with Judith. Mrs. Fontaine was pointing to a tall plant, engrossed in explaining something to the younger woman.

"Hello," Alexandra called. Both women looked at her, Mrs. Fontaine with a smile and Judith with a blank expression. Alexandra put her medical bag on the ground and held out both her hands to Judith. "I was sorry to hear about your father. This must be a troubling and confusing time for you."

At first Judith seemed not to know what to do, but she eventually placed both her hands in Alexandra's. Her hands felt limp and lifeless, and her expression still showed no emotion. She mumbled something that sounded like, *yes.*

"I've convinced Judith to stay with me at least for a while," Mrs. Fontaine said.

"A wonderful idea," Alexandra said. "I'm happy to see you're well enough to be up and about." She looked at Judith. "Are you able to sleep? I can give you a powder if you need it. Or if you would like to talk—"

"Talk? What good will it do? It won't bring him back." Judith turned toward Alexandra. "This. . .this thing he's done. . . He did it out of remorse for what he did to those men."

Alexandra glanced at Mrs. Fontaine, who nodded as if to confirm she'd heard Judith's theory about her father's guilt.

"Let's go inside and have a cup of tea," Mrs. Fontaine said. "It will make you feel better, Judith. Come along."

When they were inside, Alexandra sat with Judith in the parlor while Mrs. Fontaine prepared the tea.

"It doesn't matter, really, whether anyone believes me now or not," Judith said. "They'll know I was right once the killings stop." Her voice still sounded lifeless.

"You are absolutely convinced your father killed those men?" Alexandra said.

"Of course."

"But in each case, there was no sign of murder. No cuts or bludgeoned heads or bodies, no pistol wounds."

"But everyone knows they were killed, don't they? The entire village is calling the deaths murder," Judith said. "Even you believe the men were murdered, Dr. Gladstone. I can see it in your eyes, hear it in your voice."

"Even if anyone or everyone believes the men were murdered, there are numerous other theories about the killings. Some say they were killed because they knew about that buried treasure in the Freemason's temple."

"Buried treasure?" Judith asked as she accepted a cup from Mrs. Fontaine.

"It's an old legend that resurfaces from time to time in the parish," Alexandra said. "I'm surprised you haven't heard it."

Judith shook her head.

"Perhaps that's because you didn't grow up here," Alexandra said, accepting a steaming cup from Mrs. Fontaine.

"Legends usually have some basis in truth," Mrs. Fontaine said.

"What do you mean?" Judith's face had grown even paler than it was before.

"The Templar treasure. There could be some basis for the legend," Mrs. Fontaine said. "The Templars were Europe's bankers at one time. Controlled most of the money in all of Europe. Some say that's why they were disbanded. Rulers and kings didn't like the idea of any group having that much power, you see."

"Of course, I know about the Templars and their money," Judith said. "What does that have to do with the Temple of the Ninth Daughter?"

"When the Templars were disbanded, and most of them killed, some of the money and other treasurers were buried in their temples," Mrs. Fontaine said. "The Temple for the Lodge of the Ninth Daughter was built over the ruins of one of the order's temples, and the treasure is said to still be there."

Judith set her tea cup on the table with trembling hands. "Why wasn't I ever told this?" she asked.

"Those of us who have lived her a long time simply take the legend for granted, since we've heard it so many times," Alexandra said. "It's one of those stories that stays buried for long periods before it resurfaces."

"My father must have known about it," Judith said.

"Of course he knew." Mrs. Fontaine turned to Alexandra. "I do wish you'd stop referring to it as a legend, Alexandra, my dear," she said. "It's certainly more than a legend. Anyway, as I said, legends almost always have some basis in truth."

"Perhaps you're right," Alexandra said.

Do you remember my telling you about the old line families?" Mrs. Fontaine asked, addressing Alexandra. "Many of them had money invested with the Templea. Some family members still grumble about the money owed them by those knights, even after seven centuries."

"Interesting," Alexandra said. "That's something I've never heard before. Do you think it could be some family member terrorizing the town dressed as a knight and murdering people?"

Mrs. Fontaine shook her head and smiled. "I don't speculate on such things, dear. When one has lived as long as I have, one hears many stories. All I can say is that, from my experience, not all of them are legend. And," she added after a slight pause, "one also learns that money is a powerful motive for all kinds of misdeeds."

"Indeed," Alexandra said as she stood. She looked at both women. "I'm happy to see that each of you is doing well. At least relatively speaking," she added as she glanced at Judith, whose face by now had regained some of its color. "And I do thank you for the tea, Mrs. Fontaine, but I must be going. I want to stop by to see Charlotte Malcolm and her new baby."

"Yes, of course," Mrs. Fontaine said. "I went to see her myself recently. Baked a meat pie for the poor child. She certainly looked as if she needed it. So pale! What a dreadful experience she had with the birth. Oh," she said, turning to Judith, "don't let it frighten you about giving birth, Judith. Most of the time it's not so dramatic."

"Certainly not," Alexandra said.

"Is woman's sole purpose to bear children? Oh, and keep her reputation in tack?"

"That's an interesting question," Alexandra said. "I wish I had time to discuss it with you."

"But of course you must go, Alexandra. I always look forward to your visits," Mrs. Fontaine said, standing as well.

"And I thank you for your concern about me, Dr. Gladstone" Judith said. "I do apologize for what must seem like strange behavior, but I'm afraid I feel a bit addled."

"Who can blame you?" Alexandra said, smiling at her. "After your father's death and the other deaths and turmoil that have settled in Newton--it's enough to make anyone feel addled."

"Oh yes, it's all so unsettling, but the constable will be home soon, and I'm certain that will restore at least a modicum of calm," Mrs. Fontaine said.

Alexandra sighed and shook her head in a weary gesture. "I wish we could be certain of that. It's really quite troubling that Constable Snow seems to have disappeared completely."

Mrs. Fontaine gave her a gentle smile and patted her shoulder. "He hasn't disappeared, my dear. In fact, I am convinced he's on his way back as we speak."

"I hope you're right," Alexandra said, marveling at how trusting the woman was when everyone else in the village was either angry or suspicious or both. Mrs. Fontaine didn't seem to be able to see the dark side of anyone.

Alexandra waved goodbye to the old woman and looked around for Zack who always waited for her outside the door of any patient she visited. He was nowhere in sight. Perhaps he'd been frightened away by the cats. She called his name and eventually saw him trotting toward her, coming from the side of the cottage. His usually white face was darkened with dirt, as were his front paws.

"Zack! What have you done?"

At the sound of Alexandra's angry voice, Zack ducked his head and tried to slink away from her, but she grabbed the scruff of his neck and led him to the side of the house. She sucked in her breath when she saw the patch of upturned soil and bits of plants scattered on the ground.

It was with considerable embarrassment that Alexandra knocked on Mrs. Fontaine's door again to tell her that Zack had destroyed part of her garden.

"I shall be happy to pay for the damage," she said after she'd shown her what Zack had done.

Mrs. Fontaine laughed. "Damage? I should say not. I was going to dig up that section anyway. Besides, it's a dog's nature to want to dig when spring weather softens the ground."

Alexandra remained embarrassed, nevertheless and couldn't get Zack away soon enough.

Three patients were waiting in the surgery by the time Alexandra returned, and she had no chance to speak with Nancy about anything except medicine for several hours. Finally, she and Nancy were able to retire to the parlor for a few minutes for a respite.

"Nancy," Alexandra said as they each sat down, "do you remember that old story of the buried treasure here in Newton? It's supposed to be in the—" Before she was able to finish the sentence, Zack stood up suddenly from his resting place in front of the fireplace and barked twice to signal that someone was at the surgery door.

"No rest for the weary," Nancy said as she rose to her feet and headed toward the surgery wing of the house. Alexandra followed close behind. She soon saw that it was Lord Dunsford in the waiting room. He stood, looking handsome and trim in his riding clothes and tapping his riding crop against his leg.

"Ah, there you are," he said when he saw Alexandra. "I thought you might be off on another emergency. How is the young mother you attended?"

"Better than she was earlier," Alexandra said. "But that's not why you're here."

"No, as a matter of fact, I came out of curiosity. I couldn't wait any longer to learn what you've found in the specimens you took during the autopsy."

"I can't be certain yet. I must do more research."

"Of course," Nicholas said. "At least there've been no more mysteriously dead Freemasons."

"No," Alexandra said, "but I was just about to tell Nancy something I heard today on my rounds that's quite interesting."

"Something related to the deaths?"

"Perhaps."

"Something about the buried treasure in Newton-upon-Sea," Nancy said, turning to Nicholas.

"Buried treasure? By all means, you must tell us,. Nicholas pulled out one of the waiting-room chairs and held it, signaling for Alexandra to sit, then did the same for Nancy before he sat himself in another chair.

"We used to talk about it when we were children. Haven't thought of it in years," Nancy said when Alexandra had relayed Mrs. Fontaine's story to them.

"Buried treasure? A curse? Sounds like a lot of rot to me," Nicholas said.

"I can't remember all the details about those old-line families you said Mrs. Fontaine mentioned," Nancy said.

"I've heard of those families," Nicholas said, "and that part isn't all legend. I believe they're just as Mrs. Fontaine described them to you—old aristocracy. They're all over Europe and England. I don't remember a Templar connection, but perhaps I've simply forgotten. I could never keep it all straight. My grandmother used to talk about them. We are supposedly descended from them, but who knows if that's true. That would be on the Forsythe side, my father's side. I believe most of my mother's family members were ruffians and thieves until the sixteenth century."

"So some of the treasure could be yours, my lord," Nancy said.

Nicholas laughed. "I'm not going to waste my time trying to collect it. What I'm more concerned about is the restless mood in Newton—after all those deaths, the entire village is in turmoil. Think of the mob trying to break into the coroner's building. And there's plenty of speculation about the horseman, too. Some even say it's Robert Snow. If he doesn't show up soon, I'm afraid the village is going to descend into complete chaos."

"Mrs. Fontaine is completely convinced that Constable Snow will return soon."

"Now how would she know that?" Nancy asked.

"Why, she doesn't know, of course. It's simply that she can't see anything but good in everyone she meets."

"Perhaps she really does know where he is and why," Nicholas said." She seems to know something about everyone in this town, even more than you, Nancy, if you'll forgive me for saying so. Mrs. Fontaine has lived in Newton-upon-Sea longer than anyone else alive, I'd wager. She probably a few secrets about. . . . Why are you blushing, Nancy? Does she know something about you?"

Alexandra put a hand on his arm. "Nicholas, please. . . ."

"Ah, you're blushing, too, my dear Alexandra. This is becoming more and more interesting."

"Don't be ridiculous, of course I'm not blushing." The truth was, Alexandra did have her own secret regarding an old lover, but as far as she knew, only Nancy was aware of the details.

"Very well," Nicholas said. He winked, making Alexandra blush even more.

Nicholas barely had time to be on his way when a sharp bark from Zack distracted the three of them. As she and Nancy made their way to the front, Alexandra was musing over

Zack's demeanor with Nicholas. He still hadn't shown his usual belligerence toward him. This time, he had done nothing more threatening than stand at attention, as if he was still assessing the situation. Could it be he'd decided to trust Nicholas as a result of his actions that night in front of the mortuary?

Once they were in the main part of the house, Nancy went to the door ,while Alexandra settled herself in the parlor, ready to see who had come to visit. From where she sat, she could see the door. Nancy opened it to Constable Snow.

Chapter 13

"God help us, it's you!" Nancy said when she saw the constable.

"I shouldn't think my presence requires intervention from the Almighty." Snow's voice was taciturn, verging on scolding. When Nancy continued to look at him with a surprised expression, he asked, "Am I to be invited in?"

"Of course, Constable," Nancy said, coming to her senses. "You're here to see Dr. Gladstone, of course. She's in the parlor."

"Good evening, Constable," Alexandra called from a few feet behind Nancy. "This is a surprise. You've been greatly missd and have been gone quite a long time."

"Be that as it may, I'm here now," he said. "I came as soon as I was summoned."

"Summoned? May I ask who summoned you? I wasn't aware anyone knew of your whereabouts." Alexandra's tone was stiff. She couldn't help but be angry with him for abandoning his duties when he was most needed.

"I've come to ask you to relay to me all that you know about the recent deaths in Newton-upon-Sea," Snow said, ignoring her questions.

Alexandra was silent for a moment, looking at him while her anger smoldered. "Very well," she said at length. "I suggest you have a seat."

"Shall I bring tea?" Nancy asked.

"That won't be necessary, Nancy. I want you to have a seat as well. You can provide the constable with any information I leave out or may be unaware of."

Snow showed no sign of contrition as he sat, listening to Alexandra and Nancy relay all of the events. Together, they told him nearly everything they knew, leaving out only that they had performed an illegal autopsy.

"First of all," Snow said when they had finished their stories, "I shall assure you that Miss Payne's father could not have possibly murdered anyone as his daughter suggests. I have known George Payne for a great number of years, and I know that he is completely incapable of killing anyone."

"Including himself?" Alexandra asked.

"I shan't speculate on that. One never knows what may bring unbearable distress to others."

"But you clearly believe his daughter was lying about her father's guilt," Alexandra said. "Why would she do such a thing? Lie about her own father?"

"She wasn't lying in the strictest sense, I suppose," Snow said, his manner as stiff as ever. "I can imagine that she believes it. Her relationship with her father was not a smooth one after her mother died. Miss Payne has always been somewhat unstable and prone to jump to conclusions unwisely."

"Has she, indeed?" Alexandra said, trying her best not to appear to be bristling.

"Yes," Snow said, pronouncing the word as if it were a final decision and not to be contested.

"So you don't believe her story that Mr. Mayhew and Mr. Fitzsimmons were her suitors? And, one might suppose, Deputy Daniel Poole as well," Alexandra said.

"I have no knowledge of who her suitors may be, nor do I believe it necessary that I do," Snow said.

"I see," Alexandra said. "Could that mean you are more inclined to believe the story of a treasure buried under the floor of the temple being a motive for murders?"

"There is no treasure buried under the floor of the temple," Snow said, accompanying his statement with a mixture of a sneer and a scoff. "I am a ast Grand Master of the Lodge of the Ninth Daughter, as was my father before me. Beyond that, I have done considerable research on the founding and history of the lodge, so I believe I am in a position to say with definitiveness that the story of a buried treasure is rubbish."

"But it's certainly possible someone could believe it's there," Alexandra said. "Possibly even kill for it."

"Many outlandish things are possible. Few are probable."

"What of the so-called knight who rides the streets of Newton-upon-Sea?" Nancy asked. She had been squirming and shifting about in her chair, eager to say something more since she'd finished her part of the story.

"You two say you saw him yourselves," Snow said, "and since you are relatively stable individuals, for females, and since there are reports of more than one sighting besides yours, I shall not be quick to discount it. As to whether it is connected to the murders or merely the act of some deranged individual, I cannot say."

"Is it only a coincidence that sightings of the horseman coincided with each of the murders?" Alexandra asked.

"I shouldn't need to tell you that I will be examining and considering every possible link to the crimes," Snow said.

"Will you also explain your long absence to the citizens of Newton-upon-Sea at some point?" Alexandra's heart pounded as she asked, knowing her question could be considered impertinent and unable to forget that he had once been her teacher.

Snow's eyes narrowed and his back straightened. "My absence was of a personal nature. Beyond that, no further explanation is warranted." With that, he stood and spoke to Nancy. "My hat and cloak, please." Then, looking down at Alexandra, who was still seated, he said, "Good night, Dr. Gladstone."

"Same odd bird that he ever was," Nancy said when he was gone.

"I should think he seemed even odder than usual," Alexandra said. "It's as if he wants to deny all that has happened here."

"Could it be his strange behavior is because he's trying to hide something?"

"Let's not jump to conclusions, Nancy," Alexandra said.

"Perhaps he was in Newton all along," Nancy said.

"I find that difficult to believe," Alexandra answered. "I fail to see how he could have been here without someone knowing about it."

"You know as well as I, how strange and secretive he's always been. Even when we were children, and he was our tutor."

Alexandra sighed. "I do admit that all of the current goings on seem strange." She paused for a moment before she spoke again. "It only adds to the mystery, does it not, that Mrs. Fontaine seemed to know that Constable Snow would be back in Newton by tonight?"

Nancy's face took on a knowing expression. "It could be she knew he was here all along. She must have known his schedule as well."

"That's not likely," Alexandra said.

"Begging your pardon, miss, but 'tis the only explanation."

Alexandra frowned. "Well. . .unless she somehow sent him a message and asked him to return."

Nancy shrugged. "You have to admit 'tis possible. As Lord Dunsford said, she's lived in Newton-upon-Sea longer than anyone else and known most of us since we were born, including Constable Snow."

"Do you also believe she knew *why* he was in London, if indeed he was?"

"'Tis possible," Nancy said and nodded.

"Then why didn't she tell someone? It would have gone a long way toward calming the mood of everyone."

Before Nancy could reply, they were both distracted by a strange moaning coming from Zack. It was only then that Alexandra noticed that he was no longer in the room with them. She called his name, but there was no response. A few seconds later, she heard another moan.

"He's not in the house," Nancy said. "He's somewhere outdoors."

"Odd," Alexandra said. "He doesn't usually like to go outdoors when it's dark. There must be something wrong."

Nancy went to the door and called for him. "He's not here in the front," Nancy said, turning to Alexandra. "He must have slipped out through the kitchen door."

Alexandra knew that was a possibility, since they often left the kitchen door open a while in the early evening, in case Rob or Artie needed entrance to the house. She ran with Nancy to the kitchen where the door was indeed open, and they heard Zack's low growling moan again. They found him outside, near the door. He was lying on his side, his feet and legs jerking.

"Dear God in heaven, he's been poisoned!" Nancy said, bending over him to watch as Alexandra forced one of his eyes open to reveal a dilated pupil.

"Help me get him inside," Alexandra said.

Together, they managed to get him inside to the surgery, but he was too heavy to be lifted up to the table. They laid him on a small rug, and Alexandra began an examination, noting his rapid breath and profuse drooling. She hurried back to the parlor where she kept a bookcase full of the medical books she'd inherited from her father. In the early days of his practice he'd served as both a physician *and* a veterinarian. Pulling a book from a shelf, she leafed through it until she found what she wanted.

Running back to the surgery, she called to Nancy. "Dover's powder!" The words were barely out of her mouth before Nancy handed her the bowl containing the mixture of ipecac and opium. The pestle was still in the bowl as she turned aside to bring a small cup of water to add to the mixture so Alexandra could pour it down Zack's throat.

Zack was convulsing again, and his drooling had become more profuse, although his moans had grown weaker. "How could he have gotten poison?" Nancy asked as she held the dog's jaws open for Alexandra to pour the mixture into his mouth. She clamped his mouth and snout, forcing him to swallow.

Alexandra could only shake her head in response to Nancy's question. She was too upset by Zack's condition to be able to speak. Possibilities ran through her mind: He could have eaten something on the streets of Newton-upon-Sea or in front of someone's house while he waited for her. He could have found something outside her own house. Someone could have poisoned him deliberately. The last scenario was the most upsetting to her. She couldn't imagine anyone deliberately poisoning Zack or any other animal.

Finally, Zack gagged and then vomited. The ipecac mixture had done its job. Now she could only hope that it was sufficient to rid Zack's body of all of the poison. He vomited a few more times, giving her even more hope. For several minutes he lay still while Nancy and Alexandra watched him closely. At last, he raised his head and seemed to indicate that he recognized both Nancy and Alexandra. However, his pupils were only slightly less dilated, and he was obviously weak, Some of the opium they had forced him to ingest had most likely cleared his body when he vomited. There probably wouldn't be enough left in his system to induce sleep, but his weakness might allow him to rest. That, both Alexandra and Nancy knew, would be the best of all remedies for him at this point.

The two of them took turns staying up with him and watching over him for several hours. He was still lethargic by morning, and Alexandra would not allow him to accompany her on her rounds. He offered no protest but continued to lie on his side, obviously ill. She left him in Nancy's care.

When she stopped at Mrs. Fontaine's house the next day for another routine check, it was Judith who answered the door. Her face was even more drawn than it had been before, and she bade her enter in a tired voice and told her Mrs. Fontaine was resting in her bedroom.

"You don't look well, Judith," Alexandra said.

"No, I suppose not." Her voice was listless. "I'm as puzzled as anyone about my own reaction to my father's death. Conflicted, actually. He was. . .obsessed, of course, and what he did was evil, but somehow, his death has affected me in a way I didn't expect."

"I understand, certainly," Alexandra said. "He was, after all, your father."

"Yes, he was my father, and though it may be hard to believe, I have some rather nice memories of him from when I was a child," she said, her voice still dull. "Our disagreements started after I was grown. That's when I asserted that I wanted control of my own life. He refused to believe he should not have a right to manipulate my entire existence. You won't be surprised to hear that he felt it his obligation—his right, actually—to take control of me until my husband could assume the responsibility."

"Yes," Alexandra said, "I understand the conflict. It's unfortunate, but I'm afraid it's pervasive in our modern society."

Judith looked down at her hands and didn't reply.

"If I may ask you another question," Alexandra said, "about Daniel Poole."

Judith raised her eyes to look at Alexandra. "Yes?"

"You said your father's motive for killing the first two men was because they were your suitors. Was Mr. Poole also your suitor?'

"Of course not. He was a married man. Surely you know the reason he died."

"You believe it was because your father somehow learned you spoke to the deputy?"

"Yes. Didn't I warn you he'd find out?"

"You did, but you thought you would be the one in danger."

Judith shook her head while tears welled in her eyes. "I was wrong, I suppose. Maybe he could never have hurt me. I don't know. I didn't know what he was capable of doing. But if he killed the first two, it seems he was capable of anything."

Alexandra shook her head. "None of us expected another death."

When Judith did no more than look down at her hands again, Alexandra added, "If you'll excuse me, I'd like to see Mrs. Fontaine."

Judith nodded and showed Alexandra to the bedroom upstairs where Mrs. Fontaine rested then returned to the parlor. Mrs. Fontaine was awake and sitting up against two pillows. All four of her cats were on the bed beside her, nestled on the embroidered counterpane. There was an old-fashioned green carpet splotched with red leaves on the floor. The furniture was of the finest mahogany, including a large wardrobe that must have been in the family for at least a century, judging from its style

"I'm sorry you're not feeling well," Alexandra said. She placed a hand on her forehead, noting that there was no apparent fever.

"Only a little tired," Mrs. Fontaine said. "My age, you know, but Judith was kind enough to stay with me a little longer."

"Thoughtful of her," Alexandra said, as she removed her stethoscope from her bag. Mrs. Fontaine's heartrate was normal, but she was pale and clammy. "Are you sleeping well?" she asked.

Mrs. Fontaine gave her a wan smile. "As we age, we develop odd sleeping habits. I may fall asleep in my chair during the day, but I stay awake most of the night. Nothing to worry about, I'm sure," she said with a dismissive wave of her hand. "Perhaps the need for sleep is not so urgent when the eternal sleep is so rapidly approaching," she added.

"I suspect you need a tonic to restore your energy," Alexandra said. "I know that would seem to contradict your need for sleep. However, my father taught me that a restorative elixir puts the body back in the proper rhythm so that sleep comes naturally."

"Oh yes, Huntington was keen on restoring the body's rhythm. I remember that well," Mrs. Fontaine said and smiled again. "Such a wise man, and it's a comfort to know he passed along some of his wisdom to you."

"Thank you," Alexandra said, noting that the lady had conceded that her father had passed on only *some* of his wisdom. Nevertheless, it was a compliment, since there were many who wouldn't admit that a woman, even his daughter, could possibly live up to the standards of their beloved Dr. Huntington Gladstone. Never mind that he had been her principal teacher in the medical profession. "I'll see that the tonic is delivered to you before the end of the day," she said.

"Thank you, my dear," Mrs. Fontaine said, leaning back against her pillows while the cat who had moved to her lap purred at a level so loud it reminded Alexandra of the constant grind of grist mills.

By the time Alexandra had replaced her stethoscope in her medical bag, Judith had re-entered the room. "Is she going to be all right?" she asked, anxiety in her voice.

"I believe so," Alexandra said, "but she needs rest." She paused for a moment and looked at each of the women. "Now, I have some news for both of you," she said. "Constable Snow has returned." There was no reaction from Mrs. Fontaine, but Judith's eyes grew wider. "Apparently, someone in the village sent for him," Alexandra said. "Do you know who that could be?" She directed her question to Mrs. Fontaine.

"He was a most secretive man," Mrs. Fontaine said, "Never divulged much to anyone. Nevertheless, he's a good man. I know that with absolute certainty."

"You're right, he's always been a bit eccentric," Alexandra said. "This recent disappearance was odd, however, even for him. Nevertheless, he's back." She turned to Judith. "He is completely convinced your father had nothing to do with the deaths of those men."

Judith grew pale again. "Of course, he would be. Constable Snow and my father enjoyed a rather close friendship."

"I wasn't aware of that," Alexandra said.

"Oh yes, they were chums," Mrs. Fontaine said, "even when they were youths." She stroked the cat in her lap, initiating an even louder purr from the cat. "I suppose the Freemason brotherhood also created a bond."

"I see," Alexandra said.

"Why would Snow come to see you first when he arrived?" Judith asked.

"He knew I had examined the bodies of those who died, with the exception of your father, of course. He only wanted to gather details from me."

"You examined all of those bodies?" Judith asked. "What a dreadful duty. You must have been appalled."

"It's part of my profession, my dear. Constable Snow often relies on my reports. There are many questions to be answered about all of these deaths."

Judith shook her head and seemed on the verge of tears. "I told you who killed all of those men. If only the two of you would listen to me."

"Now, now, Judith, calm yourself, dear child," Mrs. Fontaine said, taking her hand from the cat's silky back long enough to reach for Judith and give her a comforting pat on her hand. "She's immensely distraught," Mrs. Fontaine said, glancing at Alexandra. "Who can blame her?"

"Who indeed?" Alexandra said and turned back to Judith. "Please do try to stay as calm as possible. I don't think you should be alone."

"She'll continue to stay with me," Mrs. Fontaine said. "It will be good for both of us."

Alexandra turned to Judith. "Will you agree to stay here a while longer?"

She nodded, looking paler than she had before.

"Very well, then, I'll be going. Send for me if either of you should need me. I'll be in my surgery the rest of the day, barring an emergency."

By the time Alexandra left Mrs. Fontaine's house, it was nearing noon, and there wasn't enough time to finish her rounds before she was compelled to be at the surgery to see patients. She would have to finish her rounds later. There were only three of her patients who should not wait until the next morning. One was Vernon Walcott, who was suffering from consumption with a bloody, frothy expectorant when he coughed. The others were Charlotte and her son, both of whom remained in weak conditions.

When she arrived at her own home, it was too late for lunch, and she expected Nancy to be in a foul mood, since whatever she had cooked would have grown cold. Nancy made no mention of lunch or anything she might have prepared when Alexandra entered through the surgery door. She was busy with a patient—a boy who had broken his arm in a fall. She finished splinting and bandaging the break, all the while assuring the boy and his mother that the break was not serious and would heal quickly.

"Zack?" Alexandra said as she walked past Nancy. She could see that he was not in his usual spot just outside the door of the hallway that led to the main house.

Nancy made a gesture with her head toward the front of the house as she finished her work with the splint and bandage. Alexandra found him in the parlor in front of the hearth. Worry stabbed at her when he did not jump to his feet and lumber toward her, wagging his tail as he usually did when he saw her. The most he could manage was to raise his head and then lick her hand when she sat on the floor next to him.

"Oh Zack!" she said as she stroked his head. "Get well. Please. You must."

He whimpered and licked her hand again then laid his head in her lap. She took the time to check his pupils and to feel for swollen glands before she stood to go to the surgery. Zack rose to his feet and followed her a few steps before he stopped and lay on the floor. Dismayed,

Alexandra went back to the surgery to see a steady flow of patients. However, while she was examining a little girl with chicken pox, the girl's smile made her follow the child's eyes to the hall doorway where she saw Zack in his usual spot. He lay on his side, sleeping

"He wants to be near us," Nancy said.

Alexandra nodded as she soothed the girl's itchy pox with chamomile. She wanted to be near him as well.

When the last patient left, and the surgery door was closed, Nancy went toward the doorway where Zack still waited. He stood when he saw her approach. His stance was wobbly, but Alexandra felt a bit of encouragement that he could stand.

Nancy seemed encouraged as well, as she rubbed the top of head. "Supper will be warmed over lunch, since you weren't here to eat it," she said over her shoulder to Alexandra. "You can wait in the parlor with Zack, since 'tis obvious he'd appreciate the attention."

"I'm afraid I can't yet give him the attention he deserves," Alexandra said. "I wasn't able to finish my rounds this morning since I spent too much time with Mrs. Fontaine and Judith. Now I must see Charlotte and her baby as well as Vernon Walcott before darkness falls."

"But you didn't have lunch. You must not go without your supper," Nancy scolded.

"I won't go without. I'll be back soon," Alexandra assured her. When Zack saw her retrieve her medical bag, he sensed that she was leaving, and he made an unsteady attempt to follow her. "Zack's not well enough to go with me," she said and glanced at Nancy. "Keep good watch over him."

"Of course, I will," Nancy said, sounding disgruntled. She was never happy when Alexandra missed a meal, and certainly not when she missed two.

Alexandra stepped out the door and walked past the stable where Artie and Rob lounged in front, trying to spin a top on an area of hard-packed earth.

"Goin' out again, are ye?" Rob called. "I'll 'ave old Lucy saddled quick-like. Want me to go wif ye? To protect ye, I means."

"No need," she answered. "And no need to saddle Lucy again. The weather is rather pleasant, and I shall enjoy the walk."

"Beggin' yer pardon, doc, I can't let ye go alone. It ain't safe." Rob was on his feet, determined to accompany her.

"No, Rob. Stay here and help Nancy see after Zack. I only have two stops to make, and neither of them is far away." Alexandra wanted no company at the moment. She craved solitude after a long, busy day.

Rob stopped before he reached her side, sensing her determination. "Whatever you say, doc, but mark what I say. It ain't a good idea."

"I'll remember that." Alexandra walked along the path leading to the road thinking she might have liked to have Zack trudging along silently in heavy, lumbering gait. He wouldn't demand conversation and would want only to be by her side. She tried to put thoughts and especially worry about him out of her mind and made her way toward her first stop—the Malcolms' place.

She was relieved to see some improvement in both mother and child. The baby was gaining weight with the help of the wet nurse. She knew, however, that neither was completely out of danger, and that she would need to look in on them often.

The sky had turned gloomy with clouds that had rolled in from the sea as she made her way toward the house where Mr. Walcott lived with his aging widow. She knew his condition would not be as encouraging as that of Charlotte and her baby. Consumption was almost always fatal, and his bloody sputum and continuously weakening condition told her he could not last long. Still, she wanted to offer him, as well as his wife, as much comfort as possible.

She was almost half a mile away from the couple's cottage when a whooshing sound startled her, and in the next moment she saw a long-bladed knife embed itself in the ground in front of her, quivering from the force of its landing. Turning her head quickly toward the wooded area at the side of the road, she saw rapid movement . In the next moment, she saw a figure—a man dressed in trousers and a farmer's hat. He had something in his hand, something that glinted in the dying light of the spring evening. Another knife!

Without meaning to, she dropped her medical bag as she hurried into the stand of trees on the opposite side of the road, hoping the man wouldn't see her. She stood with her back pressed against an oak tree, her heart galloping in her chest, her breath coming in short, terrified gasps. She heard leaves rustling as something—the knife-wielding man—crashed through the trees coming ever closer

Chapter 14

The sound of footsteps crushing last year's dried leaves that had never been raked, grew louder. Alexandra knew with certainty the man with the knife would soon find her if she stayed where she stood, only partially hidden by the tree. If she ran, he would see her, since the trees were widely spaced.

Fear clawed at her. It was impossible to think rationally, and her reaction was pure instinct.

She ran.

The hem of her skirts picked up leaves and dampness, encumbering her. She could not run fast enough. Even her own body seemed to be weighing her down. The sound of footsteps behind her quickened and grew even louder.

The remains of an ancient hedgerow loomed in front of her, and she ran toward it, hoping she was agile enough to jump over it. Hiking her skirts in front, she lunged, one leg stretched in front of her, the other straightened behind her as much as her heavy skirts would allow.

It surprised her that she cleared the hedgerow, but it surprised her even more as she found herself rolling down a steep embankment. Pebbles dug into her hands and face. Branches and roots tore her stockings and cut her legs. When, at last, she stopped tumbling, she was too stunned to stand at first. Her face, arms, and legs stung where blood seeped from her scraped skin and mingled with soil and fine pebbles. Glancing up, she saw a figure looming over the edge of the embankment. Dark clouds obscured the dying light enough that it was impossible to clearly distinguish details of the face, but she knew it had to be the man who had followed her. A rush of fright brought with it enough energy to clear her mind and make her forget the fire of abrasions on her skin.

She shot to her feet, and felt a tormenting stab at her lower leg. She would not allow herself to think it could be broken, and she tried to run. This time a white-hot rod of agony twisted in her leg, making anything beyond stumbling impossible. But she kept going. Her only hope was that it would take the man pursuing her long enough to make his way down the embankment that she would have time to escape.

Escape where? She tried to force herself to ignore the torture of her leg. Yet, all she could do was drag her aching limb and continue on—to what and to where, she had no idea; she only knew she had to keep moving. Her foot caught on something, bringing her to a sudden halt. For a fraction of a second she was aware of her body pitching forward and of her bloodied hands in front of her, trying to break her fall.

Then only darkness.

Nancy made no attempt to deny her anger at first. The meal she had prepared was growing cold for the second time. She had been waiting for Alexandra so they could have their meal together, and now she was hungry. She'd already given Artie and Rob their supper, and she'd fed Zack. Or she'd tried to feed him. He still had no interest in his food. At least he was standing, although he was still wobbly. She was desperately worried about him, and it seemed to her now, in her tired and famished state, that it was immensely unfair of Miss Alex to leave her to care for him alone. Something could happen. Anything. She wouldn't be able to abide it if Zack collapsed or died while she was alone with him.

After a few minutes, she sat down at the table and helped herself to a serving of potatoes and cut off a generous slice of the sausage she'd boiled. After a few mouthfuls had settled in her stomach, she felt ashamed. She should know, after all these years with Miss Alex, that if the doctor was late, there would be good reason. Either Charlotte or Mr. Walcott had worsened, and she had to take extra time with them. Or, perhaps she'd been called away to another patient. Eventually, Alexandra would send word to Nancy by someone.

Nancy ate the rest of her meal quietly and without agitation, and there was no more self-pity. However, by the time she'd finished and washed her plate, she felt a nagging worry. She should have heard from Miss Alex by now. In the past, she'd always sent someone as soon as possible to let her know why she was late.

Zack, as well, sensed that something wasn't right. He kept his ears raised in constant alert and paced the floor—not with as much vigor as usual, for he had to take frequent rests.

"I know, Zack, 'tis late, and she's still not here," Nancy said. "What could have happened to her?"

Zack howled—a mournful sound that deeply disturbed Nancy.

She paced the floor with Zack for several minutes until he collapsed in front of the kitchen hearth, unable to stand any longer. She sat next to him and took his head in her lap.

"Don't give up now, Zack. We must be strong together." She was still speaking to him in soothing tones, hoping they would dampen her own worries when she heard a knock at the kitchen door. Zack lifted his head briefly, then laid it in her lap again, a signal that whoever was at the door was of no interest to him. "Who is it?" Nancy called toward the door.

"'Tis us, Nance. She ain't come back yet."

She laid Zack's head on the floor and rose to open the door for Rob and Artie.

"They's something wrong, I fear," Rob said. "She ought to be home by now. 'Tis full dark, and she ain't sent nobody to tell us why she ain't here."

Artie stood behind Rob, his face pale with worry.

"I know, Rob," Nancy said. "We should have heard something by now."

"Why ain't she back?" Artie asked. "Rob told her not to go alone. We shoulda went wif 'er, like Rob said."

Nancy shook her head. "I don't know why she's not here, but I'm certain we'll hear from her soon." She forced her voice and demeanor to remain as calm as possible in front of the boys.

Zack, recognizing the boys, struggled to his feet and ambled toward them.

"'E's still sick, ain't 'e?" Artie said, placing a hand on Zack's head.

"I'm afraid so. Dr. Gladstone thinks he may have been poisoned."

"Who would do such evil?" Artie asked.

"If only I knew!" Nancy said. Zack's illness, and now Miss Alex not showing up—it was almost too much to bear. She could feel a headache coming on, but she dare not take one of the powders Miss Alex often prescribed. It would make her sleepy, and she had to be awake in case Miss Alex was in trouble and needed her, or in case Zack took a turn for the worse.

"I think I needs to go out and search for the doc," Rob said.

Nancy looked at him in silence for a moment. "As much as I hate to send you out at night, I'm afraid you're right. But I worry about you going out alone."

"'Course I'm goin' alone," Rob said. "Ye got to stay here wif ol' Zack, and Artie's too young, but don't ye worry. I knows what I'm doin', I does."

"I ain't too young!" Artie protested. "I'll go if I wants."

Nancy frowned, unable to decide what to do. "All right," she said finally. "You go on, Rob. Take a lantern, and saddle Lucy and ride her. Dr. Gladstone was on her way to the Malcolm house and then to Vernon Walcott's place. Go to the Malcolms' first and ask if they've seen her, and then—"

"I knows where she went. I knows what to do!" Rob was impatient, ready to leave.

"Go on, then," Nancy said. "Artie and I will stay here and care for Zack."

"Sorry to cross ye, Nance, but I ain't stayin'," Artie said.

"Don't argue with me, young man!" Nancy warned. She watched Rob hurry away, and turned back to Artie. "Take Zack to the parlor and sit with him in front of the hearth. You know his favorite spot. Go on now! Do as I say. I have some work to do in the surgery."

Artie frowned and hesitated for a moment before he led Zack toward the parlor.

"Rub his head," Nancy called to him. "He likes that." She watched Artie move away with slumped shoulders. "Go on!" she said again. "I think I can find an extra scone and some jam for us to have when I finish my chores."

Artie gave her a quick glance over his shoulder and continued toward the parlor. Nancy was too worried about Alexandra to enjoy even a moment of self-satisfaction for coming up with the bribe.

It took her no more than twenty minutes to put away vials and bottles and medicine, remove the sheet from the examination table, and replace it with a fresh one. They were all chores she should have done earlier, but she'd been too distracted by worry. The time to fetch the scones and spread them with jam took even less time. When she walked into the parlor carrying two plates and the scones, neither Artie nor Zack were there.

The tremendous roaring sound of a train approaching was the first thing Alexandra noticed, but the sound grew fainter. That meant the train was leaving, not approaching.

It wasn't a train.

There was no *click-clack* of metal wheels on metal tracks, only a steady roar. Was she near the sea? She opened her eyes and saw nothing but darkness. She was in bed. Not her own bed, but one filled with rocks and soil and. . .and what? Something cold and slimy slithered along her leg. She cried out, at the same time kicking her leg in an attempt to shake the thing off her.

The thing flew up into the air briefly then hit the floor with a thump. No, it wasn't the floor. It was packed earth. She was lying on the ground. She heard a sound. *Swish, whish*. The thing was moving among the dried leaves. Moving away? Or moving toward her? Get away from it! She must get away from it, but when she tried to move, a pain bit into her leg.

She remembered now. She'd hurt her leg. The tibia, and it was painful to move. She passed her hand along her leg. The skin wasn't broken, except for an abrasion, but she could feel the break in the bone beneath her skin. .How had it happened? She couldn't remember. Couldn't remember why she was lying on the ground at night. Couldn't remember why her mouth and lips felt dry. She tried to moisten her lips with her tongue and tasted dust.

While she sputtered and spat, she heard the swishing sound again. The slimy, slithering creature was coming back. She tried to kick with both of her legs to keep it away, but she could manage to move only one leg. It seemed to work. The rustling in the leaves had stopped.

No. It was still moving. On her foot. Upward on her injured leg.

Sliding, gliding, creeping.

She tried to shove it away with her other foot. The heel of her shoe dug into her leg, and at the same time, the thing twined itself around her ankle. She screamed, but the darkness around her was so heavy, the sound was muffled.

"Artie! Zack! Where are you?" Worry slunk into Nancy's veins and clotted, making it hard to move as she tried to hurry through the house, upstairs and down again, calling their names. She stepped out the door and was met with a cool dampness that freed her a little from the heavy feeling. She called their names again and waited, but there was still no response. Running to the stables, she fumbled in the darkness until she found the second lantern, always hung next to the one Rob had taken. She would have to run back to the house, through the darkness to find a lucifer to strike and light the oil-soaked wick of the lantern. If only Zack were there, she would feel at least a little more secure fumbling around in the darkness. But he wasn't there. And neither was Miss Alex, or Artie, or Rob. For a moment, she felt a gush of anger at all of them for leaving her abandoned and fearful. She shook her head to force away the irrational emotions and lit the lantern. She found her cloak and hurried out of the house, holding the lantern in front of her.

Standing there, holding the light, she felt a moment of uncertainty. Should she go toward the Malcolms' cottage, as she'd told Rob to do? Artie was probably on the way there now. With Zack? The dog would try to follow, wouldn't he? Would he be too sick and fall by the wayside? Perhaps it would be wiser not to try to look for any of them, but to wait at the house in case one of them came back and needed her. Of course, that's what she should do. She should wait. That was the wise choice.

Fear and worry kept wisdom from taking root, and she hurried down the road toward the Malcolm cottage, the lantern swinging at her side as she ran. She called their names: *Miss Alex, Artie, Rob, Zack.* The effort of shouting and running at the same time stole breath from her lungs, and she gave up using her voice and ran silently until she reached the Malcolm's house.

The dwelling sat hunched against the darkness with no welcoming lights from the windows. That could only mean Alexandra wasn't there. Perhaps they'd seen her, though. She had to stop and ask.

A groggy and disgruntled Samuel, dressed in his nightshirt, came to the door when Nancy knocked. Behind him the baby cried. "Oh, 'tis you! How many more of ye are comin' tonight?" he said when he saw her.

Nancy was puzzled by his response. "How many. . .?"

"The bloke what works fer the doc. 'E came here looking for 'er. I told 'im she's been gone from here coupla hours, and I'm tellin' ye the same. All this knockin' at the door in the middle of the night wakes the babe. Ye hears that, don't ye? All that cryin'? And if ye think 'tis easy to get 'im back to sleep, ye don't know nothin'."

"Give him a bit of pap, and he'll go back to sleep," Nancy said as she turned away.

"Pap? Wot's pap?" Samuel called to her.

"Soak a bit of bread in milk 'til 'tis soft. Boil the milk first," she answered.

"She's all right, ain't she? The doc, I mean," he called again. "Ain't a good sign that nobody can find 'er."

"No," she said. "Not a good sign at all."

The next stop would be the Wolcott cottage. All of the lanes in the neighborhood were darkened, without a single light burning in a window. It gave her little hope that she would find

Alexandra there, but she knew of nothing else to do except keep walking. Not only was there no lighted cottage to walk toward, but there was no hint of Artie or Zack or Rob along the way. She felt energy and hope draining from her.

She'd walked only a few yards when she heard something in the distance. It took her a moment to realize it was the sound of hooves hitting the ground in a rapid and rhythmical pattern. She kept walking, holding her lantern high, and hoping that the rider would stop and give her word of Alexandra and the others.

"Ho there!" she called as the rider charged toward her. "Slow down, please. I would ask you a question."

Horse and rider ignored her call. She tried to move to avoid a collision, but as she veered away, the man on the horse turned toward her again. Seeing the flash of a knife blade, Nancy fell to the ground when the horse's powerful shoulder muscles struck her body.

Light and darkness swirled around her. A woman appeared in the mists of her vision. An angel?

Chapter 15

Alexandra smelled the rain before she felt the soft, teasing mist. It was fresh and earthy, the scent of spring, but it was accompanied by a slashing knife of wind that cut through her clothes and into her flesh.

The wind and the ache in her leg made her forget for a moment the horrors of the night before. The pain was referring itself into her foot and ankle now. She sat up suddenly, her hands flaying at her legs when she remembered the slimy, slithering thing she had battled in the darkness. There was nothing there on her legs, none of the things she had imagined—snakes, slimy rodents, unnamed crawling creatures. There was only her torn stockings, ripped skirt, and clumps of dirt and mud.

When she heard the rustling in the leaves again, she knew she hadn't imagined the creature, but a surge of pain in her leg made her forget for a moment. Her head whirled with dizziness, and for a moment she thought she would be sick. She lowered herself down onto her bed of dirt and pebbles and exposed roots, all of it dampened and cold from the rain. She lay there for a moment, trying to will away the sharp agony, trying to remember what had happened and why she had spent the night in such misery. Looking around, she remembered the fall, remembered the steep slope of the ravine. She was at the bottom of a canyon of sorts where no one could see her. Wouldn't Nancy and the boys call out to her as they searched? Or had they called, and she hadn't heard? She knew she'd slept part of the night. Now, she had to force herself to stand and find a way out.

A spasm grabbed her leg and bit into it with long, jagged teeth when she tried to lift herself. Her body felt abnormally heavy. She settled back to a sitting position and attempted another self-examination of her leg. Skin and tissue were swollen and tender, making it impossible to confirm her initial diagnosis of a fracture. She lifted herself slightly so she could manipulate her leg, and another, even more violent crescendo of pain came, accompanied by a moment of nausea.

She needed to force the broken ends of the bone together, and then stabilize it. Nancy always helped her with this procedure, and she usually gave the patient laudanum to dull the senses before she began. She would have the luxury of neither laudanum nor an assistant this time. Using both her hands, she pressed the upper and lower sections of her tibia, turning it slightly and manipulating it in an attempt to get the two ends joined as one might do a broken table leg, yet trying not to exert enough pressure to cause another break. Everything around her spun again, and she felt herself slumping forward as the world grew dark for a few seconds. With great effort, she pulled herself back to consciousness and pushed the bone pieces again while sweat, mixed with the mist of rain ran down her head and into her eyes. She vomited once before she convinced herself that the bones were joined. Leaning back against the side of the embankment, she took in gulps of air until the pain subsided. It never let go of her completely, but there was enough of a respite to allow her to concentrate on the next step. The fractured limb must be splinted to keep it from breaking apart again.

Searching the space around her, she pushed away pebbles, twigs, and dried leaves as she looked for a suitable piece of wood. She picked up a rounded stick, too thin to be of use, but when she started to throw it away it moved.

The snake!

It twisted itself around her hand. It was an adder! Her father had taught her to recognize the deadly viper by its big, flat head.

She screamed. Flung it away.

It landed a few feet out from her and slithered away.

She was almost too frightened to move, but she forced herself to examine her hand an arm, looking for signs of the penetration of fangs, the release of deadly poison into her veins. There was nothing on her body except dirt and debris, but she searched again, trying to push away the horror she felt.

For several seconds, she sat, stiff and unmoving, too stunned and frightened to do anything else. Finally, she forced herself to search again for something to use as a splint, this time poking at the debris with a slender twig and hoping nothing would again move under the leaves. There was bound to be a broken branch that had fallen from the trees above the ravine that would serve her purpose.

When at last she found one she thought would do, her next problem was to find how to secure it in place. She had no bandages. It took only a moment for her to realize that of course she had bandages. The petticoats and skirt that had made running difficult and that had done their part in causing her fall would redeem themselves now. She tore a strip of white cotton from the bottom of her top petticoat, and then another and another and did the same with the bottom petticoat. The dress she wore was made of a light-weight wool flannel that would be sturdy enough to hold the bandages in place.

By the time she had wrapped the leg several times and used the wool flannel as a final wrap, she was sweating. Her leg throbbed, as did her head, and wave after wave of nausea returned. A weak dawn peeked over a distant horizon and advanced with slow, timid caution.

Finally, it overruled the mist, but not before it had left her drenched. An overwhelming surge of fatigue pulsated from her insides, and she leaned against the side of the embankment once again.

She slept. There was no way to know how long, but she forced herself awake and tried to call out for help. She called for Nancy, Artie, Rob, and Zack. Her voice was weak, and her mouth so dry her tongue seemed uncommonly thick. The effort to speak was too great. She gave in to exhaustion once more and slumped to the ground.

When she awoke, the snake was there again, wet, slithering, this time moving against her face and her mouth.

Nicholas had already retired to his bedroom where he was reading when he heard a commotion downstairs. At least two people were shouting in unusually loud voices. Walls and doors in the centuries-old house at Montmarsh were thick and solid so that sound didn't penetrate them easily. When he could actually hear a fracas going on, it clearly bore investigating.

Throwing on a dressing gown, he hurried downstairs. Along with the sound of scuffling, he heard Stokes' voice, much louder than usual, and the vociferous screech of a young boy.

"Stokes! Is something wrong?" Nicholas called, just as he rounded the curve of the staircase and saw his butler and the boy. "Artie?" he said, surprised. "What are you doing here?"

"I'm terribly sorry, my lord," Stokes said. "I tried to contain the noise and the disturbance so it wouldn't awaken you, but the young hoodlum insisted that he see you. I was doing my best to keep him—"

"It's all right, Stokes, I know the boy. Something's wrong, or he wouldn't be here."

"She's disappeared, and she ain't sent word back to us like she always does," Artie screeched, " so Rob went lookin' all by hisself, 'cause Nance wouldn't let me go, but I went anyways, wif Zack. Snuck away, we did, 'cause I knowed you'd come help, and good as Rob is, 'e ain't got no carriage or no fast horse like ye has, me lord, but Zack turned back 'cause 'e's sick. Poisoned, the doc says, and if 'e dies the doc won't never get over it, if she ain't dead already, so you got to 'elp us, me lord, that's wot I was tryin' to tell the bloke what opened the door, but—"

"Artie! Artie! Slow down, I can't make heads or tails of what you're trying to tell me. Who has disappeared, and who has been poisoned?"

"Doc Gladstone." Artie was near tears.

"Doctor Gladstone has been poisoned?"

"I'm terribly sorry, my lord," Stokes said again. "Clearly the boy isn't making sense. I'm afraid his sort starts imbibing spirits at a young age. Please, my lord, go back to bed, and I'll see to it that he leaves—"

Nicholas barked at Stokes, ignoring his protective attitude. "Have my carriage readied!"

"Best take yer 'orse," Artie said. "'T'would be faster."

"We'll need the carriage to transport Dr. Gladstone," Nicholas said. "You know where she is, I assume?"

"No, me lord."

"Then how do you know she's been poisoned?"

"She ain't the one wot's poisoned. She's the one wot disappeared, and we're all afeard she's kilt."

Nicholas could hear his own blood rushing in his pounding head, but he forced himself to be calm. He'd dealt with difficult and confused clients and witnesses in his law practice. The trouble was that he'd never dealt with one when it involved someone he cared for as deeply as he cared for Alexandra Gladstone.

"All right," he said with as much calm as he could manage. "First tell me how you know the doctor has disappeared."

"'Cause she didn't come home tonight after she went to see them sick people, and when she knows she has to be late, she always gets word to us somehow. Then it got plumb dark, and we still didn't hear nothin'."

Nicholas pulled the story from Artie, little by little, including the fact that Zack was sick, and Nancy and Alexandra thought he might have been poisoned, and that he had turned back when Artie left for Montmarsh.

"Who would do such a thing? Poison a dog?" Nicholas was already on his way toward the stairway. He would go up and change clothes.

"I ain't fer knowin' that, me lord, but maybe t'was the same person wot kilt the doc."

Nicholas felt as if his heart had dropped from his chest, and he stopped, part-way up the stairs. "You don't know that for certain, do you? That she's dead, I mean."

"Don't know nothin' fer certain," Artie said, looking forlorn.

Nicholas dressed quickly, and by the time he was downstairs again, the groom was waiting outside the door with the carriage. Nicholas scooped Artie up and placed him in the seat and got in beside him. "We'll stop by the doctor's house first, in case she's returned. If she's still not there, we'll try to retrace her steps, since you say you know where the two patients she was going to visit live."

It was a two-mile ride to the Gladstone house, but they made it in record time. When they arrived, the first thing Nicholas noticed was that there were no lights burning in either the surgery or in the main part of the house.

"Ain't like Nance to go to bed when the doc's gone," Artie said. "Maybe she's back. Maybe she ain't dead or disappeared."

Nicholas jumped from the carriage, followed by Artie, and pounded on the door for several seconds, calling out to Nancy and Alexandra, but there was no answer. "Was Nancy here when you left?" Nicholas asked Artie.

"She was, me lord."

"And she told you to come for me?"

Artie was silent.

"You snuck away," Nicholas said.

Artie hesitated again. "Had to. I had to tell ye so's ye could find 'er."

"Nancy must have been beside herself when she discovered you were gone."

"But I took ol' Zack. She knowed 'ed watch out fer me."

"You said he left you," Nicholas said. "Said he went home because he was sick, but he's not here. If he were, we'd certainly hear his bark."

"I called for 'im to come back to me when 'e left me. Called 'im over and over, but 'e just kept chuggin' on with that heavy ol' walk 'e has. Ye knows how 'e does. 'E was goin' back home. Lookin' for the doc, I guess. But 'e ain't here. Maybe 'e died," Artie said, his voice choked.

"Let's not jump to conclusions," Nicholas said, although the possibility that it could be true not only for Zack, but for Alexandra and Nancy and Rob as well, was already stalking him.

"Jump wot?" Artie asked.

"Never mind, Nicholas said. "Get back in the carriage. Our job is to find all of them."

"Ye thinks we can find 'em? All of 'em."

"Of course," Nicholas lied. He urged the horses forward. "We'll retrace her route. Go to the patient nearest to the house and see if she ever made it there."

"That must be wot Rob done. 'E's smart like that."

"Nancy may have done the same," Nicholas said, as much to himself as to Artie.

"Yup," Artie said. "Nance ain't missin' too much in the way o' smarts."

Nicholas was silent for a long time, trying to decide on the best plan for the search. The moonless night would make it difficult under the best of circumstances, and the lighted lanterns at the front of the carriage did little to coax away the darkness.

"Turn here," Artie said.

It took a moment for Nicholas to realize they had come to a crossroads.

"Here?" Nicholas asked, as he gave the reins a pull to guide the horses to the left.

"No, t'other way," Artie said. "They's a house up that way where that girl lives that the doc had to cut the baby out of 'er."

Nicholas pulled the horses to a stop. "She would have gone there first. That makes sense. And Nancy and Rob would have most likely gone there as well."

"Yup," Artie said.

Nicholas was silent for another moment. "We'll start at what was supposed to be the end of her journey and work our way back this way," Nicholas said. "No use going over plowed ground."

"We ain't got time for no plowin'," Artie said. "Anyhow, it's too dark to plow."

"You are certainly correct," Nicholas said. "Now, do you know the way to the other patient's house?"

"Ol' Vern? 'Course, I does. Ye goes down that road there. The one you started down a minute ago. 'Tain't too far, but 'taint too close, neither."

"You're exceedingly helpful, Artie." Nicholas aimed the carriage down what he hoped was the right road. Except for the feeble glare of the lanterns on the carriage, the only light was from the pinpoint stars. Though they populated the heavens profusely, they did little to illuminate the world around them. Trees and brush tangled themselves together at the sides of the lane, menacing, waiting in the darkness. Not a single light shown from a cottage along the way.

They drove on in the oppressive cloister for several minutes until Nicholas spied something ahead. A light, pathetic against the thickness of night, appeared in front of them. Nicholas stared at the blinking image. When Artie sucked in his breath, Nicholas knew he had seen it as well.

"Wot is it?" Artie whispered, as if the far-away shimmer might hear him and disappear.

"Not sure," Nicholas said, also in a whisper. He urged the horses onward. When he was a few yards closer, he called, "Who goes there?"

"'Tis a person ye thinks?" said Artie. "Not a ghost or a demon?"

"A person, yes, I think so. I believe he's carrying a lantern."

"He? Could be a woman."

"I don't believe so," Nicholas said.

"Not Nance or the doc?"

"It appears to be someone riding a horse, judging by how high the light is above the ground." Nicholas called out several more times, asking the unknown figure to identify himself or herself. Finally, an answer came.

"Who goes there yerself?"

"Rob!" Artie cried and tried to stand up in the carriage, but Nicholas pushed back with his arm, forcing him to sit.

"Is that you, Rob?" Nicholas called.

"I heard Artie. Who is it yer wif, Artie?"

"'Tis me and Lord Dunsworth," Artie shouted.

The light of Rob's lantern bounced in an irregular pattern as he spurred the horse he rode toward the carriage. "By god, I was hopin' that's who ye was," he said as he came upon the carriage and held his lantern high to discern their faces. "I fear they's somethin' terrible wot happened."

Nicholas felt his chest tighten. "Something terrible? What, exactly, do you mean?"

"I found 'er medicine bag, but I ain't found no sign of 'er. Sam Malcolm says she was at their 'ouse and took a look at 'is wife and babe. Ol' Vern never seen 'er, though 'e was expectin' 'er. Found 'er medicine bag, I did, 'tween the Malcolms's 'ouse and ol' Vern's place."

"If she dropped her bag, someone or something must have frightened her, Nicholas said. "She'd never leave her medicine bag unattended," Nicholas said.

"I knows that, same as ye does," Rob said. "Been lookin' fer 'er all over the place, I has. Ain't found 'er as ye can see. Somethin' terrible happened, I knows it!"

"Have you by any chance seen Nancy?" Nicholas asked.

"Nancy? Why, she's home wif Zack, I'm guessin'. Left the two of 'em and Artie there together."

"She ain't there." Artie said. "We can't find 'er, and Zack's runned away."

"Ol' Zack? Naw, he'd never do that."

"I'm afraid it's true," Nicholas said. "They're all three missing, Dr. Gladstone, Nancy, and Zack."

Rob shouted his anger and fear. "Damn and hellfire! They was all there when I left. Artie, you best tell me wot happened, boy."

Artie relayed the story of his leaving and of Zack's disappearance. "Then Nance was gone when I gets back to the 'ouse," he said, sounding sheepish.

"I ought to wallop ye good," Rob said. "Ye was supposed to all stay there where you was safe. If I know Nance, she struck out to look fer ye, and she got into some kind o' trouble, and 'tis all your fault, boy."

"I didn't mean nothin' bad to happen," Artie said, his voice trembling with the tears he was trying not to shed.

"Ye ain't got no sense, so I'm gonna knock some sense into ye," Rob said, about to dismount.

"Calm yourself!" Nicholas commanded. "Artie only did what he thought he had to do, same as you. For that matter, you ought to be glad he went off to find me. Now there are more of us to search."

"Don't matter how many they is, 'cause we don't know where to look." Rob sounded tired, and Nicholas thought he detected a tremble in Rob's voice as well.

"I think it best we wait until morning, since we can't do much good in the dark," Nicholas said. "At first light, we'll search in a grid pattern, and we'll get Constable Snow and as many others as we can to help us."

"By first light, they'll all three be dead," Rob said, sounding wearier than ever. "I ain't givin' up 'til I finds 'em. Just got to go back to the stable and get 't'other lantern. This un's outta fuel. And I got to put poor ol Lucy up for the night. She's had all she can take. I'll do the walkin' this time."

"You'll be wasting your time to go back for the other lantern," Nicholas said. "It's not in the stable. Nancy must have taken it when she left."

"Then I'll lift one from somebody's barn." Rob had already started up the road, on his way to steal a lantern.

Nicholas watched Rob, feeling conflicted, as the boy and the mare disappeared into the night. He was as eager as Rob was to keep looking until they found them, even if he knew waiting until first light was by far the more prudent choice.

"Lor'," Artie said, shivering in the damp air, "I just hope they ain't all dead. If they is, 'twill be me own fault."

Chapter 16

As Rob rode away, Nicholas heard a familiar sound that startled him at first. It was a dog barking. Zack's bark!

He'd moved the carriage only a few yards when he heard the sound of Lucy's hoof beats. It was hardly more than a minute before Rob rode Lucy back to the carriage.

"Ol Zack!" he said. "Mayhap he's found 'em. We got to look for 'em. Follow the sound o' ol Zack's bark."

"But we can't find him without light," Nicholas said. "Yours has run out of fuel, and I can't take the carriage into those brambles."

"Well, sure as the fires o' hell, I'm goin' to try," Rob said.

"Don't be a fool," Nicholas said. "Didn't you just see how hard it is to find your way anywhere in this darkness?"

"Call me a fool if ye will, but if that's ol' Zack and he found 'em, I ain't leavin' them out there to. . . ." He trailed off as he apparently noticed the same thing Nicholas had—that Zack was no longer barking. It would be impossible to follow a sound that wasn't there.

"Get in," Nicholas said. "But tie Lucy to the back first."

Rob hesitated for a few seconds before he complied. When Lucy was secured, he grabbed the side of the moving carriage and hoisted himself into the seat, maneuvering himself next to Artie.

They rode in silence until they reached the road leading to the Gladstone house. Nicholas picked up the reins and tried to lead the horses toward the house. "I'll leave the two of you here and go back to Montmarsh for a lantern before I go back to search," Nicholas said.

"You ain't leavin' me nowhere, Dunsford." Rob's voice was snarling. Artie, by this time, had fallen asleep, leaning his head on Rob's shoulder.

Nicholas looked at Rob, knowing he couldn't leave him at home without a fight. Without another word, he dropped the reins again, and gave the horses their heads to move toward Montmarsh and their own stable. He didn't want to keep pushing them hard because they'd moved at a furious pace through most of the night. The horses walked an agonizingly slow gait up the hill toward the mansion. It was not until they were almost there that they accelerated to a brisk trot. Nicholas could make out the dark mass of the grand house, and he could see lights glowing in the front hall. Stokes must have waited up for him.

A stable boy carrying a lantern appeared out of nowhere and followed the carriage as Nicholas drove it to the walkway leading to the front door of Montmarsh. "You're a welcome sight, my lord," the stable boy said. "We was all worried at this late hour."

"Feed and stable the mare I'm trailing," Nicholas said. "Then I shall need another pair of horses as well as two more lanterns for the front of the carriage and an extra lantern to take along. Make sure they're all full of oil."

"You going out again, my lord?"

"I am," Nicholas said.

"'Tis late," the stable boy protested.

"It is indeed," Nicholas said. He disembarked the carriage, along with Rob, and reached for Artie to carry him inside.

Stokes met him at the door, clearly alarmed to see him with the boy in his arms.

"Lord Dunsford, what have we here? Is the child ill?"

"Not ill, Stokes, just exhausted. See that he's put to bed, and feed him if he awakes. I know he'll be hungry."

"My lord, I'm afraid I don't know. . . . What I mean is, I have no experience with—"

"For God's sake, Stokes, get Pickwick up here. She'll know what to do."

"Of course," Stokes said and hurried away to find Mrs. Pickwick, the cook. Nicholas was often criticized by his mother, Lady Forsythe, for not keeping a full staff at Montmarsh. However, since he was not there full time, he found that Pickwick, the stable crew, and an overseer were sufficient. He'd taken to bringing Stokes along to Montmarsh only recently.

While he waited for Stokes to fetch Pickwick, a pleasant, motherly woman who was good friends with Nancy and equally reliable, Nicholas carried Artie into the library and settled him on one of the sofas with a pillow under his head. He turned to Rob, who had followed him.

"Wait here with Artie until Pickwick arrives," Nicholas said. "She'll provide you with something to eat, even if Artie doesn't awaken enough to eat. You know Pickwick, don't you?"

Rob nodded. "Knows 'er, all right. Knows 'er good as I does Nance. Comes to the surgery to gossip with Nance, she does."

"Yes, of course," Nicholas said. "Now, stay here and help take care of young Artie. I'll be back as soon as I find them."

"I'm goin' wif ye," Rob said.

"I need you to stay here and take care of Artie." Nicholas turned quickly and left the room, making sure to lock the door so Rob wouldn't follow. He met Stokes in the front hall.

"Not going out again, are you, my lord?"

"Yes. Dr. Gladstone and her maid are missing. It's threatening rain now. I must find them as quickly as possible before the weather gets even worse."

Stokes wore a troubled look on his face. "But, my lord—"

"No time to argue, Stokes. Every minute counts." Nicholas moved quickly toward the door.

"I wasn't going to argue, sir," Stokes said. "I merely want to suggest that you change into dry clothes."

Nicholas started to protest, but Stokes's remark made him remember his soggy clothing. Wearing something dry, along with a substantial raincoat, would likely aid his effort. "Very well, but we must hurry."

"Forgive me, my lord, but I'm sure you know I'm well-practiced at hurrying."

Stokes had already started upstairs, taking them two at a time. Nicholas knew his butler was right about his adeptness at moving quickly in a crisis.

Within a few minutes Nicholas came down the stairs, still buttoning his own shirt. He hadn't waited for Stokes's help. Nevertheless, Stokes slipped a cape over his shoulders as protection against the rain just as he left the house. He was pleased to see the carriage waiting with fresh horses and brightly burning lanterns just as he had requested.

For several minutes, he drove the horses harder than he knew he should have before he stopped at a crossroads, trying to remember which route he had taken before. He was grateful the rain had stopped, but there was a chill in the air. Winter was still battling with spring for dominance. He pulled his cape tighter and turned the carriage on the path he was almost certain he had taken in his initial search. He pulled the horses to a stop just after he started the turn.

He heard something.

Not a bark, as he'd hoped, or a human voice, but a distant rhythmical, thumping sound. Within seconds he recognized it as the sound of an approaching rider. He hesitated, not certain whether it would be friend or foe. Ultimately, he decided it was best that he go on with his mission and once again started in the direction he had gone earlier. He rode for several minutes when he heard Zack's barking, as before.

He reined in the horses to listen closer, so he could determine the direction from which the sound came. While stopped, he heard again the *thud, thud, thud* and knew it was approaching hoof beats. Closer now. So close, in fact, that the carriage horses were sniffing the air and dancing in place. Nicholas wasn't sure whether their reaction was because they recognized the approaching horse or because they did not. Nevertheless, he urged them forward. Only a moment later he heard shouting.

He kept the carriage and horses moving forward. The approaching rider came even closer, and Nicholas heard him shout again at the same time he heard another of Zack's barks. He didn't stop the carriage, but the fast horse behind him was soon next to him.

"Damn it, Rob!"

"Ye heard the bark?"

"I heard it. That's one of my horses you're riding, and one of my saddles you're sitting in."

"It's Zack's bark all right. We got to ride toward it."

"You can't take a horse through those brambles."

Rob dismounted. "Then we'll walk. Give me one o' them lanterns."

"I told you to stay with Artie."

"He's sleepin' like a baby, and Pickwick will watch 'im like 'e was 'er own."

"Damn it, Rob!"

"Yeah, I knows."

"I ought to—"

"Come on, me lord, ye ain't got time to be mad at me. Hear that? 'Tis Zack."

Rob had already started making his way through the brambles. Nicholas followed, but soon caught up with him, the two of them following Zack's barks. By the time they reached the embankment and saw the huge Newfoundland standing at the top, the first weak hint of dawn was creeping across the edge of the sky.

Zack hurried toward Nicholas with his familiar awkward gait, but instead of snarling and nipping at his heels the way he usually did, he grabbed the edge of his cape and pulled him.

Alexandra lay on the wet ground, her hair and clothing soaked with rain. Something was curled in her hair.

"My God!" Nicholas said as he looked down.

"'Tis a serpeant!" Rob whispered, as if he were afraid of awakening the creature.

"We've got to get it away from her," Nicholas said. He scrambled down the embankment, followed by Rob, who carried the lantern, while Zack remained at the top.

"Careful, me lord. 'Tis an adder. If ye wakes it, the thing could bite her."

Nicholas hesitated, uncertain for a moment of what to do. He saw a long stick on the ground next to Alexandra and picked it up. Gambling that the morning was cool enough that the cold-blooded animal could not move quickly, he slipped the stick under the snake's curled body and lifted it, and then, with a quick movement, flung it over the top of the embankment.

"By God, ye, done it," Rob said.

Nicholas knelt beside Alexandra and held the lantern next to her, not certain whether she was dead or alive. There was something tied to her leg.

"Gaw!" Rob said, coming up behind him. "She's dead, ain't she?"

Nicholas took her hand in his. It was cold, but not the waxy cold of death. At the same time he heard her moan. "She's not dead," he said. "We've got to get her back to the carriage." By this time Zack had laid down beside Alexandra, his head on her chest.

"Ol Zack's still sick," Rob said.

"Thank goodness he was well enough to guide us to Dr. Gladstone," Nicholas said. "Getting her out of here's not going to be easy, though."

"She's bad hurt," Rob said.

Nicholas lifted her into his arms. She moaned again as he moved her but didn't open her eyes.

"How we gonna git 'er up that bank?" Rob asked.

"Take my cape," Nicholas said, shrugging it off his shoulders. "Spread it out, and I'll lift her onto it. You take the corners of one end, and I'll take the other. We'll use it as a sling gurney to get her out."

Rob made his way up the side first, still holding the lantern. He snuffed the flame before he set it down, since it was now light enough that they wouldn't need it as a beacon at the top. He slid himself down the embankment again to aid Nicholas. The two of them walked sideways up the side of the ravine with the makeshift gurney. Zack barked encouragement from the top. Alexandra remained silent as they began the hard slog upward. Nicholas knew she had awakened, hearing a cry of pain when they almost dropped her.

Once they reached the carriage, the two of them lifted her into position in the front with her injured leg extended.

"Nancy," she said. "Nancy will know how to help me."

"I'll ride ahead," Rob said, as he mounted the horse he'd taken from Montmarsh. "Nance will probably be back by now. I'll tell her to get ready."

"Be back by now? Where is she?" Alexandra's words were slurred. She sounded more puzzled than worried.

"We've all been out searching for you," Nicholas said, trying to convince himself that Nancy would, indeed, be back by now.

"Oh," Alexandra said. "Sorry. Didn't mean to. . . ."

"Of course not," Nicholas agreed. "Do you feel up telling me what happened to you?"

"Fell down that steep. . . Broke my tibia," she said, as the carriage started forward. Zack ambled alongside, keeping as close to Alexandra as possible. "Someone with a knife. . . ." she said wearily.

"A knife? My God!"

"Where's my bag?" Alexandra said, making a sudden frantic search all around her. "My medical bag. Where is it?"

"Rob found it," Nicholas said. "It's safe at Montmarsh."

"How did it get to—?"

"Before I explain that, I want you to tell me who was following you and why. And why did he have a knife?"

"Don't know," she said. "There were snakes." She shivered as she sat beside him. "And then you came," she said. "Never been so glad to see anyone in my life."

"And I, you," Nicholas said.

Alexandra said no more. Nicholas glanced at her face and saw, in the weak purple predawn light that it was pale and contorted with pain. His first inclination was to urge the horses to move faster, but he restrained the urge, knowing it would only make the ride rougher and cause her even more discomfort.

They rode in silence for several minutes before Nicholas was able to make out two shadowy figures in the distance. He recognized the horse from his own stable that Rob was riding and a few seconds later, the white gelding Constable Snow always rode. He kept the carriage moving at a steady pace forward while the two horsemen advanced toward him at a faster rate. Their approach concerned him. He suspected it meant that Nancy had not yet returned.

"Me lord!" Rob shouted from a distance.

Nicholas responded with a wave of his hand, hoping the two of them could see it in the dim light. He didn't want to answer with a shout of his own. Alexandra appeared to have dozed off, her head resting against his shoulder, and he didn't want to wake her. Nevertheless, she sat up with a start when the sound of the horses became more pronounced.

"Lord Dunsford," Constable Snow said when he was close enough. "You must turn your carriage around toward Foulness."

"Foulness? That's almost an hour away. Dr. Gladstone needs help immediately."

"I know. Young Rob told me," Snow said, his voice tense, "but that's the location of the nearest doctor."

Nicholas started to protest that Nancy could provide the service needed, but he stopped himself, not wanting to mention it aloud for Alexandra to hear should she awaken. His effort was wasted. Alexandra lifted her head from his shoulder.

"No," she said. Her voice sounded even more strained than it had before. "Nancy can do what needs. . . ." Her voice trailed off, making it clear that she was in too much pain to speak.

"I'm afraid that's not possible," Snow said. "Nancy is missing."

Alexandra's eyes widened. "Missing?" she asked. She was obviously in a state of confusion as a result of her ordeal.

"We will begin a search for her immediately," Snow barked. "What you must do is get your leg seen to as soon as possible."

Nicholas had already pulled the horses into a turn before Alexandra could protest more. Zack, seeing the carriage turn, barked a confused protest.

"Rob!" Nicholas shouted. "See to the dog. He's not well enough to follow."

Rob dismounted quickly and threw his arms around Zack's neck. The big dog did his best to free himself, but Rob held on firmly as Zack used his considerable strength to try to shake free. He was even able to drag Rob a short distance.

As they rode away, Nicholas could hear Zack's alarmed bark. He wanted to be with his injured mistress. In time he heard a mournful howl as the horses increased the distance between them.

Chapter 17

A woman with two mouths and no eyes smiled at Alexandra. The woman dissolved into the shape of horse twisted in a circle. There was a droning sound as if a thousand bees were buzzing. The sound grew louder and louder before it stopped abruptly.

Alexandra opened her eyes and heard someone speak. "She's waking up!" It was a voice she didn't recognize.

"Her eyes look quite odd. Pupils extraordinarily dilated." She knew that voice. It belonged to someone called Nicholas. Or Lord Something-or-Other. Now he was gone from her vision. There were only dancing lights in front of her

"She'll come around presently, but it takes a while. I gave her a mixture of ipecacuanha and opium as an anesthesia so I could examine her leg and make certain it was set properly. Only a small dose, though. As you can see, she's already awakening." The voice came from one of the dancing lights—a green one that had grown an uncommonly large mouth.

"Alexandra?"

She turned her head toward the sound of her name. It was Nicholas. The features of his face began to take shape in the green light.

"Alexandra, my dear. You're going to be all right."

"Yes, my darling, I'm going to be quite all right," she said. She felt someone squeeze her hand and brush her forehead with a kiss. Then she slept.

She had no way of knowing how long she slept, but when she awakened, she saw Nicholas seated in a chair next to the bed. She couldn't remember at first why she was here in this strange room. When she tried to get up, a jolt of pain in her leg brought back a memory of her injured limb and her attempt to make a splint from a tree branch.

"Where am I?" Her lips and throat were parched, making it impossible to form words properly.

"You're in Dr. Abercrombie's surgery." Nicholas said.

"Abercrombie? I have heard of. . . . Do I know him?"

"He's a physician here in Foulness. I brought you here so he could examine your leg. Apparently you did a fine job setting it yourself. Abercrombie was quite impressed."

"Rob said he was a quack." She was surprised to hear herself using that word.

"Don't worry, I've checked his credentials. He's quite capable of setting a broken leg," Nicholas said.

"Why didn't you allow Nancy. . . ?" Her voice trailed off.

"Try not to be upset. Constable Snow is searching for her."

She tried to get up. A sickening pain in her head momentarily blinded her and forced her down again.

"Alexandra, please. . . ." She felt Nicholas's hand encircling hers, and his other hand gently easing her shoulders down.

"I must find her," Alexandra said. "That person with the knife. Did he attack her?"

Then the room revolved before it floated away. She saw nothing after that except visions of Nancy with a knife stuck in her chest.

Nicholas held a cup of cold water to her lips. "Ah, you're awake again. You were having nightmares—crying and mumbling. Here, drink this."

The sky had begun to darken before Alexandra felt herself awake again. She asked Nicholas to go over in detail everything that had happened, and she, in turn, was able to tell him everything she remembered.

By the time they had finished their accounting, Dr. Abercrombie had entered. He was wearing a white apron over his suit, and a stethoscope hung around his neck. The apron was soiled with blood. "You're awake, I see, but with considerable pain, I would imagine."

"Some, yes." Alexandra knew if she complained too much, she'd be confined longer.

"Allow me to compliment you on the splint and bandage you somehow managed to provide for yourself. I dare say, not many of us could do that."

Alexandra thanked him for the compliment and started to ask him to help her up, but Dr. Abercrombie interrupted. "Your early attention quite possible ensured that you will be able to walk on the leg again, albeit with a limp."

"I fully intend to walk normally," Alexandra said.

"My dear, you must be grateful to walk at all, whether it be normal or not."

"I believe I should attempt to stand by tomorrow. Without weight on the leg, of course."

"Certainly not!" Abercrombie said. "You are a physician, and if you received the proper training, you should know a broken leg demands complete bed rest for several weeks."

"Of course I know that is the standard procedure," Alexandra said, sounding defensive, "but my experience has taught me that early, brief attempts at standing help overall health. I've also observed that some weight on the leg after a few weeks helps strengthen supporting muscles."

"While you are in my care, you will be treated, not according to someone's dubious experiments, but by standard and proven medical procedures," Abercrombie said in a voice devoid of sympathy.

Alexandra pressed her lips together to keep from arguing, telling herself that the more she protested, the more difficult her stay would be. At the same time, she knew with certainty that her stay would be no longer than a few more hours after dawn arrived.

"I understand that I am in Foulness," Alexandra said, hoping a change of subject would diffuse the tension she'd created.

"You are indeed." Abercrombie's tone was one of superiority.

"Were you by any chance acquainted with the late George Payne?"

Abercrombie lifted his chin and nose higher. "Why do you ask?"

"His daughter, Judith, lives in Newton-upon-Sea."

"Indeed she does," Abercrombie said. "I know her well. Knew her father equally well, if you must know. Tragic! So tragic!"

"His suicide, you mean," Nicholas said.

"My good man, it was most certainly not a suicide." Abercrombie scolded.

Nicholas shot Alexandra a quick glance. "Not a suicide?"

"I have not seen the body, mind you," Abercrombie said. "It was our local law enforcement who proclaimed the death a suicide, but that was most certainly a mistake. I should have been called. Constables and the like are usually ill trained in such matters, as are some doctors, I might add."

"May I ask how you've come to this conclusion that it was not suicide? And how your constable came to his conclusion that it was?" Nicholas asked. The questions had come so quickly, Alexandra sensed that he was attempting to make sure she didn't speak up and cause another argument. She was content to stay out of it if it would hasten her opportunity to leave, and she knew Nicholas would ask all of the questions she would have asked and more. She had his training as a barrister to thank for that.

"As I said, I knew the family well. George Payne was an honorable man. He would never have stooped to the cowardly act of suicide. He was murdered."

"By your own admission, you didn't see the body," Nicholas said. "How—"

Abercrombie raised his voice a decibel higher, "George Payne was a loyal Freemason, a Grand Master. Why, he was even wearing his Masonic apron when he died. Smeared with his own blood, the constable said." Abercrombie snorted, a derisive sound. "How he came to the conclusion of suicide is beyond me, since there was said to be no wound. The constable claims he took poison and vomited the blood. Rubbish, I say. Complete rubbish. I should have been called to examine the body."

Nicholas frowned. "Even his own daughter believes it was suicide."

Abercrombie closed his eyes as if he were struggling to be tolerant of the ignorance surrounding him. "His daughter is female. She is, by that very nature, hysterical and unreliable in her judgment. I believe Mr. Payne would have agreed with me on that point. They didn't get along at all, you know."

"Do you know the nature of their disagreements?" Alexandra asked, regretting it when she saw the acrimonious glance Abercrombie shot in her direction.

"I do, but I refuse to go into detail, since I am not one to gossip. Suffice it to say that young Judith was quite rebellious, a most disagreeable characteristic of any off-spring, and particularly a daughter. She insisted upon making all of her own decisions. Everything from what she wore and where she lived to whom she married. Quite like her mother, I believe. In short, the rift between father and daughter was, in this case, quite clearly the daughter's fault."

"Surely you don't think the disagreement was so severe as to bring about murder," Nicholas said.

Abercrombie stared at Nicholas, speechless for a few seconds before he spoke. "She is unruly, Mr. Forsythe, but she is not insane, and she most certainly could not be a murderess."

Alexandra noticed that the doctor had addressed Nicholas as Mr. Forsythe rather than Lord Dunsford. That was obviously the way Nicholas had introduced himself. Nicholas seemed to have a sixth sense as to when the title would serve him and when it would not. He was, nevertheless, unruffled by Abercrombie's superior manner.

"Are there others, then, who might be suspect?" Nicholas asked.

Abercrombie snapped at him. "Of course there are others. Aren't there always? Brother Payne's unfortunate financial situation put him in contact with some of those in the seamy side of life, although he himself was from the best of families. One never knows about some classes, does one?"

"Could you suspect anyone in Newton-upon-Sea?"

"Perhaps. I know there was. . . . Well, never mind. Almost anyone could be suspect, I suppose. With the exception of most members of the brotherhood, including myself. We are a small lodge, compared to the Ninth Daughter in Newton-upon-Sea, but quite honorable and devoted to each other. Are you a member of the Ninth Daughter, by any chance?"

"I spend most of my time in London, where I have a law practice," Nicholas said with careful evasiveness.

"A solicitor?"

"Yes," Nicholas said, not bothering to add that he was also a barrister.

"Indeed," Abercrombie said. "Perhaps you could answer a question I have concerning property I own. There is a minor dispute over a boundary, you see and. . . ."

Abercrombie went on to explain a rather complicated matter to Nicholas, seeking his free advice. It was at least an hour later, and Alexandra was growing tired before he left with an apology that she would have to stay in the examination room overnight since there was no hospital in Foulness.

"I shall have to find you someone in a private residence who will be willing to take you in," he said.

Rob watched as the morning light sifting through the window grew stronger and stronger. He had slept little during the night, but Artie, who shared the sleeping quarters above the Gladstone stables, was sleeping soundly, his arm thrown across the wide expanse of Zack's back. The dog hadn't wanted to go up to the stable living quarters at first, but they had finally persuaded him with the help of a sizable and meaty beef bone Rob took from the kitchen. The bone had been cooked in a stew and was still unspoiled and had a few scraps of meat still attached. He'd taken the stew, along with a bit of bread and leftover sausage for himself and Artie.

Rob was reasonably certain both Nancy and Dr. Gladstone knew he could enter the house at will, even when the door was locked, but they'd never protested because he'd never misused that ability. They knew he'd learned questionable skills such as how to enter a house undetected when he was trying to survive on the streets and along the docks of Newton-upon-Sea. That learning experience had begun when he was younger than Artie was now. Nance and the doc knew all about it. Yet, both of the women trusted him. He'd never do anything to betray that trust, but he'd never let Zack or Artie go hungry, either.

Zack hadn't slept particularly well during the night, either. All night long, he kept going to the window to look out as if to see if Nance and the doc were finally home. At least he'd devoured that bone with enthusiasm. A good sign that he was getting over his sick spell, Rob thought. Poisoned, the doc said. Who would do a thing like that? Some no-good bloody bastard, that's who.

Zack stirred, twitching his feet a little then raised his head. He looked at Rob a few seconds before he maneuvered himself into a standing position. He looked around, sniffing the air for the scent of the two women who cared for him.

Rob felt fairly confident that Dr. Gladstone would be well cared for. Lord Dunsford would see to that. He seemed like a decent bloke, and it was clear he fancied the doc. Nance was another matter. He was worried about her something awful. She'd never stay away this long, unless something bad had happened. Like being kidnapped or dead. Rob pushed those thoughts from his mind and tried to think of what he should do.

The simple answer was to go find her but where to start looking? Artie said she must have left the house to search for the doc. She knew where the doc was supposed to be, so she would have covered the same ground he and Lord Dunsford had covered looking for both of them. They'd searched a lot of territory, and there'd been no sign of Nance. If there was no body, mayhap she'd been kidnapped after all. That made no sense, though, because there was no reason to kidnap her. The only thing that made sense was to go search for her again If Zack was well enough, he could take him along. That nose of his was worth the dog's weight in gold when it came to finding things.

Besides not knowing where to start looking, there was another problem: Artie. Rob saw that he was still asleep, his hair touseled, his arm still flung out where Zack had been. Sleep made his face appear even younger than his years. It was hard to believe he was already eight years old. It seemed to Rob it was only yesterday when he found him shivering in the rain and trying to stay dry in an old broken-down shipping crate that had washed ashore.

"What ye doin' here?" Rob had asked him.

"Nuffin," the boy had answered.

"Git on home. Yer mum'll be worried."

Rob had already started to walk away when Artie said, "Got no mum."

Rob paused for a second. He hadn't wanted to care what happened to the boy, even if he didn't have a mother. He had problems enough of his own. In spite of himself, he'd turned around and pulled the boy out of the crate and got him to the empty shed at the end of a row of docks where there were other boys who lived on the streets trying to stay warm and dry.

Artie had eventually told Rob as much of his short life story as he could remember. His mother, he said, worked in a factory at night, but he didn't know what kind of factory. She was with him during the day, although she was sick with a bloody cough. Rob concluded that she had consumption. He'd picked up a few bits of information from the doc. Artie's mother had told him he was five years old, and she was the one who told someone to go to his father when she died. Artie had never known he had a father. That didn't surprise Rob, since he'd never met or heard anything about his own father.

Someone Artie didn't know brought him from London to Newton-upon-Sea where his father was supposed to live. When he couldn't find the man, he'd simply abandoned Artie at the docks where his father was said to work.

Rob's own story was different in that he remembered his mother all too well— how she'd beat him and broke his arm once. That arm was still crooked. Too bad the doc couldn't have set it for him back then. He remembered his mother mostly drunk, mostly with men he didn't know. He'd finally run away and ended up in Newton-upon-Sea. He'd learned to survive by theft, mostly. He was just teaching Artie some of those skills when the doc came along and got both of them out of some trouble. It was Nance that took in him and Artie. Hired them as stable boys without even asking the doc. Not that the doc ever protested. She was a good 'un, she was. Now they had plenty of food, a dry, warm place to sleep, and no one ever beat them. They did have to learn reading and writing which was dreadful at first, but now Rob looked forward to school, although he still pretended he didn't.

Sometimes he also pretended he didn't like taking care of Artie. Truth was, he'd grown so fond of the boy, he couldn't imagine not having him around to care for. That didn't mean the chap didn't cause him problems, though. Like now. He couldn't just leave him alone while he searched for Nancy. Even if Artie didn't end up hurting himself somehow, he couldn't trust him to *stay* at home. He'd do something boneheaded. Like last time when he'd slipped away from Nance and caused even more trouble than they had already.

"What ye doin', Rob?" Artie had just opened his eyes and seen Rob staring at him. He was sitting up, rubbing his eyes, and his little-boy voice sounded even younger now that it was hoarse with sleep. It embarrassed Rob that the boy had seen him like that—staring at him like a bloody granny.

"None o' yer business wot I'm doin'."

Artie looked around the little room. "Where's Zack?"

"In the corner behind that old saddle, chewin' on a bone."

"Well enough to eat, is 'e? That's good, ain't it?"

Rob didn't respond at first. He was busy slicing the sausage he'd warmed up on the small stove they had in their room. "Here's some breakfast if ye wants it," he said, sliding a plate filled with the sausage and some of the stew onto a table. He watched Artie eat for a while before he spoke again. "Don't know what to do wif ye while I'm out."

"Out? Where ye goin'?'

"Got to look fer Nance, ye dumb bloke."

Artie turned the plate up to lick it. "Don't have to do nothin' wif me. I'm goin' too."

"No you ain't. You'll slow me down."

"Won't slow ye down, ye dumb bloke. We'll ride Lucy."

Of course they could ride Lucy, Rob thought. Why hadn't he thought of that? Lucy was small, but she was strong enough to carry the weight of the two of them, and she'd had plenty of time to rest after her last jaunt. The little bugger was smarter than he thought.

Rob rushed Artie through his breakfast while he saddled Lucy and found a few provisions to take along. In less than an hour, they were both astride the mare and on their way. Zack moved along beside them, more sluggish than usual, but he refused to leave their side. It troubled Rob that he still had no solid plan for the search, but he knew he couldn't simply wait at home.

There was no reason to cover the same ground they'd covered before. They'd searched around the Malcolm and Wolcott cottages and into the wooded area where they found the doc. This time they crossed the road leading to Foulness, an hour's ride away along the coastline. It was scary to think about Nancy wandering along the coast. Could she have fallen from a rock into the sea and drowned? And what about the doc? Sure, she was being watched over by the earl, but what if things were out of the earl's hands? Rob knew most people survived a broken leg, but he'd also heard of people who'd died after such an injury. Something could go wrong inside a body and you'd never know it until it was too late. He chided himself. Bad thoughts, he believed, could lead to a bad outcome. He urged Lucy on toward the rocky coast line.

It was not easy for the little mare to walk through the rocks, but they kept going, asking fishermen along the route if they'd seen any sign of the small, blonde woman dressed in plain blue dress over the last few days. No one had seen her, and no one had heard of anyone drowning or a body washing ashore.

Rob kept a watch on the sun as it moved down the western sky. When it dropped far enough, he turned Lucy around.

"We got to get home 'fore it gits dark," he told Artie. "I ain't fer bein' out in the night again."

Artie didn't protest but clung tight to Rob's waist as they made the unsteady ride across the uneven ground. Zack followed along with no protest. It seemed he was back to his old self again. Just as they reached the road to Foulness, the dog stopped.

"Come on, Zack. Keep movin'," Rob called.

The dog sniffed the air, barked once, and started up the road, moving away from Newton-upon-Sea and the Gladstone house.

"Ol' Zack knows somethin'," Artie said. "They's somethin' on that road."

Without replying, Rob turned Lucy around to follow Zack.

"Wot ye think e's after?" Artie asked.

"Don't know." Rob was a bit apprehensive and at the same time, excited. Could it possibly be Nance? Or was it more trouble?

Within a few minutes, Rob and Artie saw what Zack had sensed. A carriage was approaching. It was hard to make out at first because of the fading light, but before long, they both knew it was Lord Dunsford's carriage. Zack knew as well and was now racing toward it. Rob urged Lucy forward.

Before long, Artie was waving his arms and shouting over Rob's shoulder. "Is that you, me lord? Is that you?"

Lord Dunsford waved back to them, and someone in the carriage waved as well. Was it Nance? No, it was the doc. And why was she riding in a carriage so soon after her accident? Rob could imagine that she'd give a patient of hers a piece of her mind for doing that.

"Did you find Nance?" Artie asked as the carriage drew closer.

"No, I'm afraid not," Lord Dunsford said as he pulled the carriage beside them.

"Nicholas, please, we must find her!" The doc's voice sounded funny, like she was in pain. No wonder at that, Rob knew.

"You'll be going to Montmarsh, my dear." Lord Dunsford's voice was firm. "The constable is searching for Nancy, and as soon as possible, I'll join him."

"But she—"

"You're going to Montmarsh where Mrs. Pickwick can see after you, and I'll hear no more protests," Lord Dunsford said. It startled Rob a little. He'd never heard anyone talk to the doc that way before. He could tell the doc didn't like it, but she wouldn't make a fuss in front of him and Artie. Instead, she turned her attention to Zack, who was standing with his front paws on the carriage, licking the doc's hand and wagging his tail in a frenzied motion.

"He seems better," Dr. Gladstone said. Rob saw her wince as she made a movement to rub Zack's head. "You've taken good care of him," she added. There was no joy in her voice or in her eyes. She was clearly worried about Nance, as they all were.

"I've got to get the doctor to Montmarsh, boys," Lord Dunsford said. "She escaped from the doctor's surgery in Foulness like a thief sneaking out of gaol. Couldn't stop her. Getting free of Pickwick's grasp will be a different matter, though. If I were one to make a wager, I'd put my money on Pickwick." He already had the carriage and horses moving forward. "You boys ride ahead and tell Pickwick to get ready for us."

Rob was glad to have a job to do. It would help him keep his mind off Nancy. He managed well until they reached Montmarsh and gave the cook the news that Lord Dunsford and Dr. Gladstone would be arriving soon, and that she was charged with taking care of the wounded doctor.

"I'll take care of her," Mrs. Pickwick said. "Had experience with that sort of thing, I have. My own son fell from the top of a hayloft and broke a leg. I know all the things to do. I'm good as Nancy at that sort of thing, I dare say. And speaking of Nancy, I take it you've not found her, have you? Otherwise, 'twould be her taking care of the doctor."

"We ain't found 'er," Artie blurted. "We looked ever'where. I fear she drowned."

Mrs. Pickwick shook her head, and her eyes clouded. "Poor Nancy's gone for good, that's for sure."

Chapter 18

The chamber pot wasn't where it was supposed to be. Nancy fumbled around searching for it, and she knew she had to find it soon, because she was going to throw up. She held it as long as she could and rushed out the door, running as far away from the house as she could before she bent over and retched, spitting out the contents of her stomach.

She straightened and looked around, feeling disoriented. There was a breeze blowing in from the sea, cool but not cold, and smelling of fish and salt. It cleared her head some, and she recognized the stables, the tree where she and Miss Alex used to play, the back of the house with the rickety staircase leading down to the basement, and behind her, the door to the kitchen.

She was home! But where had she been? She started a slow walk toward the surgery door. She was weak, and the walk seemed to take forever. When at last she reached the entrance, she realized she was hungry. The kitchen seemed too far away, however, so she sat down to rest. She was in the waiting area, and just beyond was the room with the examination table, vials of medicine, and all of Miss Alex's instruments and files. Where was Miss Alex? Of course! The doctor had to be making her morning rounds. How could she have forgotten that after all the years they'd worked together?

It took her a moment for Nancy to realize that she had spent the night on the examination table, and that was why she couldn't find the chamber pot she kept under her bed. How strange it was to sleep on the examination table, and fully dressed as well! She stood up again, feeling even more confused.

If she was hungry, then everyone else must be as well. She would go to the kitchen and cook. . . cook what? Breakfast? Lunch? Something for tea? She hurried to the parlor to look at the clock that always sat on the mantel. It had stopped, the pendulum as still as death. She could wind the clock, but she had no way of knowing the correct time. Was it morning, as she had at first thought? Perhaps if she ate something, she could regain her senses.

The familiar look of the kitchen gave her a sense of relief. There was the heavy metal range, the fender, the fire irons, the wash tubs, the table. She frowned when she saw the loaf of bread that had been left on the table, along with crumbs scattered around. An army of ants marched in straight lines to and from the crumbs. Someone had been in her kitchen! Most likely Rob and Artie. She'd give them a proper scolding.

Forgetting her hunger, she went to the kitchen door and stepped out to walk to the stables where she'd most likely find the boys. She saw them immediately, only they weren't in the stables. They were just riding up on Lucy with Zack following along.

"What are the two of you about? Riding Lucy, are you? Without permission, I dare say. You're due a thrashing if you ask me, and where is--?"

"Nance! Oh, Nance!" Artie jumped from the mare and ran toward her, throwing his arms around her.

"You're home!" Rob said at the same time. "For the love o' God, you're home!" He looked as if he might want to throw his arms around her as well, but he held back.

"Of course, I'm home. Why wouldn't I be?" Nancy pried Artie's arms from around her. "If you think that will get you leniency for what you've done to my kitchen. . . ." She couldn't continue because Rob had both her hands and was twirling her around in a crazy dance while he laughed.

"I knowed you'd show up," he said. "Yer too full o' pluck to let 'em git the best of ye." Zack danced around her as well, barking with maniacal joy.

"Zack!" Nancy finally pulled herself away from Rob. "'Tis good to see you're no longer sick. I thought. . . ." She stopped mid-sentence, remembering how she and Miss Alex had given him a purge because they thought he'd eaten poison. She'd left him in Artie's care while she went to search for Miss Alex. But why had she been searching for her? And where was the doctor now?

She glanced at both of the boys, feeling confused all over again. "I think I need to talk to you," she said slowly because she wasn't sure how could explain the blank spots in her mind.

"We needs to talk to ye also, Nance," Rob said. "To my way of thinkin', ye got a lot to answer for."

Nancy opened her mouth, prepared to scold him again for such impertinence. Instead, she took a breath and said, "Let's go to the kitchen. There must be something there we can eat."

"Ain't much o' nothin'," Artie said. "We et most of it."

"The word is *ate,* Artie, not *et,* and how many times do I have to tell you not to use the word *ain't*? Oh, never mind," she said before he had a chance to reply. "Let's go to the kitchen. Perhaps I can find at least a little something."

The boys were more than eager to follow her and endured another scolding for leaving the bread out, but they urged her to tell them where she'd been while she prepared porridge for them.

"Where I've been? Why I've been here, of course, where else. . ." Her voice trailed off. She couldn't have been at the house all along. Too much had happened that she didn't remember.

"Ye went to look fer the doc," Artie prompted. "Ye left me here wif ol' Zack, only I didn't stay, I. . .well, ner mind that. Remember? Ye went to look fer the doc."

Nancy stirred the porridge silently, her mind racing as she tried to remember. "I went to look for Miss Alex," she said slowly. "Yes, I think I did. She didn't come home, and . . . ." She stopped stirring and turned around quickly to face the boys. "She didn't come home. Where is she? Is she. . . ?"

"She's goin' to be all right," Rob said. "She's at Montmarsh now."

Nancy frowned. "Why is she at Montmarsh?"

Rob breathed a frustrated sigh. "All right," he said. "I sees ye ain't rememberin' much, so I'll tell ye what I knows."

He related the story of the search for Alexandra, how Zack found her first with a broken leg, and how he and Lord Dunsford had finally found her.

"Lord Dunsford had to take her to Foulness to a doc there, and now she's at Montmarsh 'cause ye wasn't around to help. The constable's out lookin' fer ye now."

"A broken leg? Dear God in heaven, how she must have suffered," Nancy said, forgetting the porridge for a moment.

"She fixed it 'erself," Artie said. "Wif a stick. She's a smart un, the doc is. Didn't have to depend on that quacky duck in Foulness."

Nancy fretted. "Oh, I should have been here."

"Don't fergit the porridge," Artie said.

Nancy turned back to the pot on the stove and stirred it again. "You said she mentioned someone with a knife," she said. "I. . .I think I saw a knife."

Rob sat up straighter. "Where?"

"In someone's hand."

"Who?" Rob persisted.

"I. . .I don't know. I was afraid I would be cut, I. . .no, I wasn't cut, but I think someone hit me, and then. . . There was someone, someone I think I know, but. . . . No, I can't remember, except she was helping me, giving me something to drink. Medicine, I think."

"She? 'Twas a woman wot hit ye?" Rob asked.

"No, not a woman. "Twas a man. He wore trousers, but a woman. . .I think I saw a woman. At first I thought 'twas Miss Alex, but. . ." Nancy rubbed her forehead where it seemed a heavy hammer was pounding away. She turned toward the cupboard, but Rob sprang from the chair where he'd been sitting next to the table and led her to another chair. Nancy saw him signal Artie with a movement of his head toward the cupboard. Artie jumped up as quickly as Rob had. He had to stand on a sideboard to reach the bowls, but he soon had three of them placed on the table, along with spoons. Rob poured porridge into each of the bowls.

"So someone was after ye, just like they was after the doc," Rob said between mouthfuls of the porridge. "A man."

"Appears that way," Nancy said, "but I know not why."

"Maybe 'twas the ghost man," Artie said. "The one what we seen on the 'orse, remember?"

"No, I don't think they were the same." Nancy reached across the table and dabbed at a spot of porridge on Artie's mouth with a napkin. "But 'twas a man who. . . ."

"You said first 'twas a woman," Rob said.

"No, I told you 'twas a man who attacked, and a woman—I think 'twas a woman—who tried to help me."

"Yer not making sense, Nance," Rob said.

Nancy said nothing. She knew she must sound irrational, and indeed she was confused about everything. It was frustrating not to be able to remember, but it would only upset her more to dwell on it. She had to get her mind on other things.

"I need to see Miss Alex," she said. "I need to make certain she's all right, that her leg was properly set."

"I tol' ye she's at Montmarsh," Rob said.

"So you did." Nancy stood and picked up the empty porridge bowls and took them to the wash basin. "I shall be leaving as soon as these bowls and the pot are washed. "

"Leave?" Artie sounded alarmed. "Where ye goin'?"

"To Montmarsh, of course."

"How ye think ye's goin' to get to Montmarsh?" Rob asked.

"I shall walk."

"Ye can't walk," Artie said. "'Tis too far."

"Of course, I can walk, and 'tis not too far. How do you think Mrs. Pickwick gets here when she comes to visit with me?"

"Well, she. . . ." Rob was at a loss for words.

"'Course Pickwick walks," Artie said. "She's twice yer size, Nance. Got all that meat on 'er, but ye's a skinny little gal. It'll wear ye down, Nance."

Nancy laughed. She was surprised how that little bit of laughter seemed to clear her head. "If I'm not back by nightfall, you'll have to come for me," she said.

"Nightfall! Ye'll be gone that long?" Rob asked, clearly disturbed.

"Of course not. I expect to be back within two or three hours, assuming everything is going well with the doctor. I was being facetious about staying until nightfall."

"Ye was bein' wot?"

"Never mind, Artie. I need you and Rob to stay here and watch after things. I don't expect many patients will show up, if any at all."

"Ye sure yer strong enough?" Rob asked. "Ye ain't been well, ye knows. And ye ain't right in the head."

"I shall be quite all right," Nancy said. "I'll take Zack with me. He'll come back and alert you if anything goes wrong. He'll be as happy to see Miss Alex as I shall be."

Within a few minutes she was on her way across the meadow toward the mansion. Zack trotted along beside her, and she looked back once to see the boys standing together and watching her as if she were going off to war.

The trek through the meadow provided a shortcut to Montmarsh. Most people, including Alexandra, used the road because it was easier for horses to walk, and the meadow would be impossible for a carriage.

She arrived at the great house in no more than half an hour, but instead of going to the front entrance, she walked around to the door at the back that was used by servants and was closer to the kitchen. Mrs. Pickwick responded to her knock. Her eyes widened when she saw who stood before her.

"Nancy!"

For a moment Nancy thought Mrs. Pickwick was going to give her a hug, although a physical display of affection was not common between them.

"May I come in, Pickwick?"

"Of course, of course." Mrs. Pickwick opened the door wider. "You're a sight to see, you are! Where have you been? What happened to you? We've all been so worried. Are you all right?"

"Yes, I'm all right, and I don't know where I've been, exactly, or what happened to me."

"Oh, Lor', Nancy, that's the way my nephew used to talk when he'd been out drinkin' all night. You haven't taken to—"

"You know me better than that, Pickwick."

Pickwick ducked her head. "'Course I do, Nancy."

"I was attacked, that's all I know. Perhaps by the same person who attacked Miss Alex. I woke up at home in the surgery, not remembering anything."

"Oh, my! Oh, my!" Mrs. Pickwick bustled around the table, pulling out a chair. "Here, sit down. You must tell me everything."

"There's nothing to tell," Nancy said. "I told you I don't remember anything. Besides, I haven't the time. I've come to see Miss Alex."

"She's resting."

"I should hope so."

Mrs. Pickwick hesitated, obviously disappointed that she wasn't going to hear anymore of Nancy's story. "I'll take you to Stokes," she said finally. "I'll tell him who you are, and he'll take you to Dr. Gladstone."

"Stokes?"

"Lord Dunsford's new butler. Not too bright if you ask me, but at least he's not as stuffy as that one his mother always brings with her when she visits."

Nancy was surprised that the earl had hired a full-time butler. He never kept more than one or two servants at Montmarsh, including Mrs. Pickwick. He'd always claimed there was no point in it, since he had no plans to live there full time. There were rumors that he'd changed his mind, mostly because Miss Alex lived in Newton-upon-Sea. Nancy wouldn't mention that now, though. She had no time for gossip with Pickwick.

Stokes was a tall man, hefty, but not fat, and well into his fifties, Nancy thought, since he was graying at the temples. He listened to Mrs. Pickwick's explanation of who Nancy was and of her relationship to Dr. Gladstone.

"Then you are the missing woman," Stokes said. "The one about whom everyone has been so concerned."

"As you can see, I'm no longer missing, Mr. Stokes, and there's no longer any reason to be concerned."

The corners of Mr. Stokes's mouth twitched slightly as he'd found what she said amusing, but he quickly gained control. "I shall see if the doctor is awake and if she's well enough to see you."

Nancy found herself wanting to tell Stokes that Miss Alex would indeed want to see her, and she would want to be awakened even if she was sleeping. She said nothing, however. She gave the butler a little nod and waited while he walked up the grand staircase.

Pickwick sniffed as he walked away. "A stickler for proper manners, that one is. Would never dream of allowing you just to go up to see her."

"I understand. 'Tis the home of an earl. Must follow protocol, mustn't we?"

"'Tis the way 'tis, I'm afraid." Pickwick hesitated for a moment before she spoke again. "Nancy, love, what happened to you whilst you was gone? You can tell me the truth, you know."

"I told you, Pickwick, I don't remember what happened. Just that I was attacked. Or hit. By a horse perhaps. I was taken away somewhere then brought back home."

"Attacked? Oh, dear. What exactly do you mean? You wasn't molested, was you?"

"Molested?"

"You know, was your honor soiled?"

Nancy gave her a look of surprise and shock. "Good lord, Pickwick! No, I was hit by something, I think, and given a potion of some kind. Something to make me sleep."

"I see," Pickwick said, her interest growing. "So, the truth is, you don't know what happened."

"No, I don't know what happened. I told you that."

"So, something like that could have happened to you, and you don't remember."

"Something like what?" Nancy asked, although she knew perfectly well where Pickwick was trying to lead her.

"You know what I mean," Pickwick said.

"No, I'm afraid I don't," Nancy said, feigning innocence.

Pickwick seemed at a loss as to how to proceed. Nancy was silent also, mischievously waiting to hear what words Pickwick would come up with next. However, Pickwick was saved by the appearance of Stokes, making his way down the stairs.

"Dr. Gladstone is most anxious to see you, miss," he said when he was standing in front of Nancy.

"Thank you, Stokes," she said. Before she started up the stairs, she turned around to speak to Pickwick. "Thank you for your help, Pickwick. We'll talk soon. Perhaps I shall remember more by then."

Pickwick's face brightened, and she gave Nancy an enthusiastic smile.

Stokes followed Nancy upstairs and led her to a room. He opened the door, and stepped in ahead of her. "Your maid is here, Miss Gladstone," he said then stood back to allow Nancy to enter.

She was surprised to see Miss Alex sitting upright, both legs dangling from the edge of the bed.

"Nancy, oh, Nancy, thank God you're safe," Alexandra said, extending both her hands toward her.

Nancy took her hands, and Alexandra brought them to her chest in an endearing gesture. "You cannot know how worried I've been about you. You must tell me everything."

"Oh, but you must first tell *me* everything. A broken leg! Why are you sitting like that? Don't you know you should have that leg elevated?"

"Certainly," Alexandra said as she struggled to stand. "I've kept it elevated, but I also know that I must try standing a little at a time."

Nancy placed both her hands on Alexandra's arms and tried to force her to sit. "But you always caution your patients to stay in bed until--"

"Yes, I know, but I've changed my mind. I think that perhaps if a patient gets out of bed and moves about sooner, with no pressure on the broken leg, of course, it brings about quicker healing."

"*Perhaps?*" Nancy sounded incredulous. "If you're not certain, then you must stay in bed. You must not take chances."

"It's a theory only, but what better opportunity to test it without doing harm to someone else?"

"You are incorrigible, Miss Alex. Isn't that the word your father used? Well, he was right, now, wasn't he? If he were alive—"

"Don't tell me what he would do if he were alive, Nancy. You know I get enough of that from all his former patients."

"Of course. I apologize. It's just that I am concerned," Nancy said.

Alexandra brought her legs up to rest on the bed. "Yes, and I am concerned about you. Now, tell me everything that happened. You first, and then I shall tell my story."

Nancy arranged pillows under Alexandra's leg to elevate it as she told her everything she'd told the boys, including about her lapse in memory and confusion when she awakened in the surgery.

Alexandra was alarmed. "You must have been given a drug."

"My conclusion, too," Nancy said. "But why?"

"I don't know, nor do I know why I was pursued and attacked on my way to visit Mr. Wolcott."

"You set your own leg?" Nancy asked. She was both amazed and somewhat alarmed. "Then you were taken to a doctor in Foulness? Some say he's not a proper doctor. What if he—"

"Feel free to examine my leg now," Alexandra said.

"I most certainly will," Nancy assured her and pushed the coverlet and nightgown away from Alexandra's injured leg. She felt along the length of the bone, examined the dressing, and pushed at the swelling in Alexandra's foot.

"Well?" Alexandra asked.

"Seems no harm's been done," Nancy said, although she was a bit loath to admit it. She didn't like the idea of a doctor she didn't know being in charge of such a procedure.

"No harm at all," Alexandra said. "Lord Dunsford inquired about Dr. Abercrombie's credentials before he would allow him to proceed."

"Speaking of Lord Dunsford," Nancy said, "where is he?"

"He's out searching for you," Alexandra said. "As soon as I heard you were here, I instructed Stokes to get word to Nicholas and the constable that you're safe."

"I'm afraid I've caused a bit of trouble," Nancy said.

"We both have," Alexandra said. "But much more troublesome is not knowing whoever it was who attacked us, or whoever killed three people in Newton. Perhaps George Payne as well."

"George Payne?" Nancy said. "I thought he killed himself."

"I wouldn't be so sure," Alexandra said.

"But I thought he was the suspect in the other murders," Nancy said.

"He may have had a motive to kill those men, but I'm not certain he killed himself."

"Who would have. . . ?" Nancy paused. "Judith? Do you think she could have killed her father?"

"One could say she had a motive."

Nancy shook her head and was about to protest that Judith Payne was most unlikely to murder anyone, and certainly not her father. Before she could speak the words, a soft knock sounded at the door.

"Who is it?" Alexandra asked.

Stokes' voice answered. "Lord Dunsworth, miss. And Constable Snow."

"Come in, please." Alexandra quickly rearranged the sheet to cover her legs.

"So good to see you, Nancy!" the earl said, going to Nancy. He gave her a quick embrace, leaving Nancy stunned. "Are you quite all right?"

"I was attacked, but I wasn't seriously hurt," Nancy said, "but I'm afraid I've been such a nuisance to everyone."

"Certainly not," Lord Dunsford responded. "The real trouble lies with someone else, I'm afraid."

"Oh?" Alexandra said before Nancy could respond.

"I'm afraid there's been yet another murder," Lord Dunsford said.

Chapter 19

Nicholas' face paled as he spoke those words. Constable Snow, as usual, showed no emotion at all.

"Oh no!" Alexandra said.

Nancy spoke at almost the same time. "When will this stop?"

"The victim was Dr. Abercrombie from Foulness," Constable Snow said. "He was killed here in Newton-upon-Sea."

"Why was he here?" Alexandra asked.

"He came here looking for me," Nicholas said. "Naturally, that makes me feel somewhat responsible for. . .for what happened to him."

"You are in no way responsible." Constable Snow's taciturn manner gave no suggestion that he was attempting to comfort Nicholas. Rather, he was simply stating a fact.

"Why would Dr. Abercrombie be looking for you?" Alexandra asked, sitting upright again.

"It seems he thought I kidnapped you and spirited you out of the hospital."

"Then I must take some responsibility," said Alexandra. "I'm the one who insisted we leave his surgery against his advice. You tried to stop me, Nic. . . .Lord Dunsford, remember?"

"The responsible party is the one who killed him," Snow plainly stated. "It is completely irrelevant why you left his surgery."

"How did you learn all of this? About Lord Dunsford being under suspicion of kidnapping, I mean," Nancy asked. Snow gave her a scathing look. He did not approve of servants joining in the conversation.

Snow's posture stiffened even more. "We've had a visit from the constable in Foulness, but that is of no importance to the matter at hand."

"There's more," Nicholas said. "The constable from Foulness is also in Newton to investigate the death of George Payne. Apparently Dr. Abercrombie finally convinced him that Mr. Payne's death was not a suicide, and is somehow connected to the murders here in Newton-upon-Sea."

Snow glared at Nicholas. "Begging your pardon, my lord, but that is police business, and this is no place to discuss the matter."

Nicholas was unperturbed by the scolding and did nothing more than glance at Alexandra with raised eyebrows as if he were dismissing Snow's protest. "In that case, let us hope the business is taken care of quickly. Let us also hope there'll be no more deaths."

Snow showed no signs of having been chastened, except for a slight drop of his chin. "Of course," he said.

"Forgive me," Nicholas said, turning back to Alexandra. "In all the excitement, I've failed to ask you how you're feeling."

"Quite well," Alexandra said. "I'm most anxious to return home. I'm quite certain I would heal even quicker there."

Nicholas frowned. "I can assure you that you would receive the best of care here at Montmarsh, and Nancy could stay on as—"

"I appreciate you generosity, my lord, but one always does better in one's own home."

"I believe she's right, my lord," Nancy said. "The doctor and I have both observed that patients fare better at home than they do in unfamiliar circumstances." Her remark elicited another disapproving glare from the constable.

Nicholas did no more than breathe a sigh of resignation. "Very well. Certainly, by now I know better than to argue with the two of you against me. I'll have the carriage readied for you, and Stokes can help me get you down the stairs. I suppose we could fashion a gurney similar to the one we used to get you up here."

"I should like to walk at least to the stairway, not entirely on my own, of course, but if I could have the support of someone--"

Nicholas interrupted her. "My dear, walking is not even to be considered."

"I insist, my lord. I will place no weight on the leg, I believe it will be better for the healing process to exercise my body at least for a short time," Alexandra said.

"But. . ." Nicholas began.

"She claims 'tis a medical experiment," Nancy said, "and as you mentioned, there's no point in arguing with her."

Alexandra was already standing and steadying herself by holding to the bedpost. "I cannot do it without help."

Nicholas and Constable Snow hurried to her, each bracing an arm for her. She took a tentative step and then another and another, hopping on one foot and holding the other so as not to put weight on the leg.

"I believe I was wrong about attempting to walk all the way to the stairs," Alexandra said. "I shall need to be lifted in that sling you mentioned before I reach them."

"Never mind that," Nicholas said and scooped her into his arms. Before Alexandra could protest, he turned to Nancy. "Hurry down ahead of us and tell Stokes to see that the carriage is ready."

Nicholas carried her in his arms all the way downstairs to the library, where he placed her on a sofa to wait for the carriage.

"I appreciate your concern about me," she said to Nicholas, "but I hope you understand that I do not wish to be treated like an invalid."

"I should like to say that because you are the doctor, you know best, but I'm afraid I can't agree with you in this case, nor can I allow—"

"No point in arguing with her, my lord," Nancy reminded him as she entered the library after informing Stokes about the carriage. "She'll do what she pleases in the long run."

"Nevertheless," Nicholas said, "I do believe--"

"No point," Nancy said again.

Nicholas took a deep breath and remained silent for the few seconds before Constable Snow appeared in the doorway. "I shall leave you in the care of Nancy and Lord Dunsford," Snow said. "I must return to the village and prepare to meet the constable from Foulness."

"I would like to examine Dr. Abercrombie's body," Alexandra said.

All three of the others in the room looked at her with surprise. Constable Snow spoke first. "Excuse me, Dr. Gladstone, but I don't believe it is advisable for you to do that. It would require your going to the mortuary."

"I shall be there later today, Constable Snow. I must have a little rest first, however."

"My dear Alexandra. . . ." Nicholas began.

"Was Dr. Abercrombie also wearing his Masonic apron when he died?" Alexandra asked.

Snow didn't answer at fist. Finally, he spoke one curt word. "Yes."

"Was it smeared with blood?" Alexandra asked.

"It was."

"The same as the other men who died."

Snow nodded, his expression stern.

"I shall examine the body," Alexandra said.

Nancy only breathed a heavy sigh.

"Are you quite sure?" Snow asked and then scowled when Alexandra assured him that she was, indeed.

Alexandra and Nancy had just finished their late-afternoon tea when Nicholas returned in his carriage to transport Alexandra to the mortuary in the village. Nancy insisted on going along to see after Alexandra.

"You can rest assured that Zack will want to come along with us as well," Nancy said. "'Tis not likely he'll let Miss Alex out of his sight after what she's been through."

"I'm still against this," Nicholas said. "I fail to see how you're going to be able to stand to do any sort of examination."

"I shall need help, of course," Alexandra said.

"She can use walking slings," Nancy said. She showed Nicholas the two long sticks that fit under each arm with slings made of leather to support weight.

"Ah yes," he said. "Those contraptions the Americans made popular during their Civil War. A sort of crutch to aid wounded soldiers, I believe. Someone should patent that, you know."

"They're not as easy to use as one might think," Nancy said, as she helped Alexandra place one under each arm. "And you must be careful," she said to Alexandra. "You must allow me on one side and Lord Dunsford on 'tother."

Alexandra didn't protest, and she allowed Nancy and Nicholas to stand on either side of her as she hobbled to the door. Zack was close behind. As soon as the door opened, he raced outside with a bellowing alarm, coming close to knocking Alexandra to her feet.

Nancy scolded him in a loud, angry voice. "Zack! Stop that!"

Zack ignored her and thumped across the grounds still with his maniacal bark. Alexandra saw what had excited him. A cat! She had never owned a cat, and they were seldom seen around her home.

"Look!" she said when she recognized the creature. "That's one of Mrs. Fontaine's cats. What's it doing so far from home?"

"There!" Nicholas cried when he saw someone hurrying away and disappearing into the long shadows of the late afternoon.

"Oh!" Alexandra cried and leaned heavier on Nicholas.

'What is it?" he asked.

"That looked like. . . . I believe that is the same figure who was chasing me when I fell."

"You said that was a man," Nicholas said.

"I'm not sure," Alexandra said.

"Could it have been a woman? Someone with cats?"

"You mean 'tis Mrs. Fontaine?" Nancy asked.

Alexandra frowned and shook her head. "I can't say."

Nicholas pushed harder. "But it's possible."

"Anything's possible," Alexandra said, regaining some of her composure. "It's too late to pursue whoever it was. Please, take me to the mortuary so I can examine the doctor's body, then I suggest we proceed on to Mrs. Fontaine's home."

Alexandra had to be helped in and out of the carriage, and she was reluctant to admit how painful it was. By the time they arrived at the mortuary, her leg was aching, but she didn't complain and managed to make her way all the way inside with the aid of the slings. Both Percy Gibbs and Constable Snow were waiting for her.

"Are you quite sure you're up to this?" Snow asked.

"Most certainly," Alexandra replied.

"Pride goeth before a fall," Percy said.

"I should like Nancy to accompany me," Alexandra said.

"Very well," Snow said. "Under the circumstances, I believe that is a wise decision. I shall accompany you as well, in case—"

"You needn't trouble yourself," Alexandra said. "I shall be quite all right."

"Nevertheless, I shall accompany you for the sake of the investigation," Snow said.

Alexandra nodded her consent, although she had hoped to examine the corpse outside of Snow's presence, since his concerns about the propriety of how much of the body she examined would most likely interfere.

As usual, Percy led all of them to the back room and then removed the sheet from the body. Alexandra noted the familiar odor as soon as the sheet was removed. Since the doctor's shirt had not yet been removed, she noted a stain on the front and leaned over to whiff the stain. It yielded another familiar scent—that of vomit.

"Dr. Foulness has been poisoned," Alexandra said.

"Are you quite certain?" Snow asked. That seemed to be his favorite question to ask her.

"I can't be absolutely sure without an examination of the organs," she admitted, "but based what I have seen when I examined the other victims, I am reasonable certain they all died of poisoning," she said.

Snow frowned. "Most unusual," he said. "Where would anyone obtain that much poison?"

"I suspect it came from someone's flower garden," she said.

Snow's face was pale. "Flower garden, indeed."

"A number of flowers commonly grown in our gardens are poisonous," Alexandra told him.

"And there are hundreds of flower gardens in Newton-upon-Sea," Snow said. "I'm afraid that doesn't pin the source down very well."

"I agree," Alexandra said. "However, it wasn't the flower that provided the poison directly. It was honey made from the flowers. The poisoned honey made each victim vomit, and it also damaged vital organs. Damaged them enough to kill." Alexandra didn't bother to tell Constable Snow that there was one garden in particular that she suspected. She didn't want another *are you quite certain* from the constable.

"Can you tell me the particular type of flower you suspect?" he asked.

Alexandra hesitated before she decided upon her answer. "Not without an examination of the organs."

"I'm afraid that's out of the question under the circumstances," Snow said.

Alexandra nodded but said nothing.

"Very well," Snow said. "Thank you for your help. I shall send a telegram to Colchester requesting the doctor to perform the procedure."

"The last time you sent a telegram requesting a doctor—Dr. Abercrombie, I believe—he never appeared in Newton-upon-Sea," Alexandra said. She didn't mention that she was glad he hadn't.

Snow looked at her, but he didn't speak. For the briefest of moments he looked as if he might be blushing, but he soon returned to himself. "I was called away before I could contact him," he said then dismissed the matter in the next sentence. "I must get to work immediately. I shall ask Lord Dunsford to help you make your way out and into the carriage."

Alexandra nodded again. As soon as he was out of the room, Nancy spoke to her.

"Called away, was he? Ha! My guess 'twas some who. . . ." She stopped speaking when she saw the stern look on Alexandra's face and changed the subject. "You know the flower in question, of course," Nancy said "'Tis oleander. I suspect, you know the source as well. 'Tis Mrs. Fontaine's garden."

"There are more than likely oleanders growing in Mrs. Fontaine's garden, but I would not be surprised to find them in other gardens in the parish."

"But honeybees. Who else has honeybees? And the cat. . . ."

"Precisely," Alexandra said.

"I'm happy that you finished so quickly," Nicholas said, striding into the room. "Now, let's get you home so you can rest."

"Nancy and I were just agreeing that we'd like you to drive us the Mrs. Fontaine's home first, as we suggested earlier," Alexandra said.

Nicholas frowned. "That's unwise."

"Not at all," Alexandra said, ignoring the pain in her leg. "I can manage well enough if you will again provide your carriage."

"Of course I'll provide the carriage, but I want you to know, I strongly object to your doing this," Nicholas said.

"Duly noted," Alexandra said as she made her way out of the back room of the mortuary and to the reception area in the front where Percy was still standing. "Thank you, Percy. I've finished my work."

"Murder, though it hath no tongue, will speak," Percy said.

"You've quoted Shakespeare this time, not the Bible," Alexandra said as she hobbled past him.

Percy spoke to Alexandra's back as she left the room. "Are you quite certain?"

By the time the carriage arrived at Mrs. Fontaine's cottage, Alexandra had given Nicholas her theory about the poisoned honey.

"You came to that conclusion simply by looking at Dr. Abercrombie's body?" he asked.

"Not entirely," she said. "It finally occurred to me that I was seeing signs of poison in Deputy Poole's organs without realizing what I was seeing at first. Then I realized that all of the victims had exhibited the same mixture of a sweet odor and a foul smell—honey and the soured contents of their stomach when they vomited. I haven't examined George Payne's body, but I suspect I'd find the same thing. Also, I've done rather a lot of reading on the matter of poisons in the medical texts my father left me. And, I've compared that information to what I was seeing under the microscope. I'll admit, it took some time for me to understand, but medical knowledge is always evolving, as you know."

"And you suspect Mrs. Fontaine? Absurd! You may as well think she's the legendary horseman!"

"Not impossible," Nancy said. "Even at her age, you'd be surprised at what the human body can do, when properly maintained over the years."

"You and Nancy thought a man was pursuing you. Who do you surmise that to be?"

"I'm not ready to say yet."

As they approached Mrs. Fontaine's cottage, Alexandra could see through one of the windows that she sat in her chair, alone but for her cats. She stared straight ahead, apparently at nothing.

When Nicholas knocked on the door, she didn't move, except to place a hand on the cat that rested in her lap.

"Mrs. Fontaine," Alexandra called, leaning heavily on her crutch after making her way to the door.

Still no verbal response.

Nicholas knocked again and this time gave the door a gentle push. Not locked, it opened slightly. "Excuse me," Nicholas said, opening the door a little wider. "May we come in?"

When she failed to reply, he repeated the question.

"If you must," she said, without getting out of her chair. She most certainly was not her usual welcoming self.

"Are you not well?" Alexandra asked.

"Well enough," she said. Alexandra thought it odd that she had not remarked on the fact that she was limping on slings. It was as if she had expected it.

"We would like to ask you some questions," Nicholas said.

Mrs. Fontaine looked at Nancy for a brief moment and seemed as if she would comment. Instead, she turned to Nicholas.

"What is it you wish to ask me, my lord?"

"Were you at the Gladstone house earlier today?" he asked.

"Yes," she said but nothing more.

Nicholas pushed harder. "May I ask why?"

Again, she didn't answer.

"Did you come hoping to see me in the surgery?" Alexandra asked. "You're in need of medication, perhaps?"

After an uncomfortably long pause, she asked, "What is the real question you want to ask?"

Alexandra took a deep breath. "We came to ask what you know about the recent rash of deaths of Freemasons in Newton-upon-Sea."

"I know a great deal," she said. It seemed for a moment that she would say no more, but then she added, "I killed them. All of them."

Chapter 20

At this shocking confession, Alexandra regarded the woman she long knew with something akin to anger. Finally she spoke. "You, who once told me God gave us life and it should be nourished in all creatures."

Mrs. Fontaine didn't respond.

Finally, Alexandra spoke again. "Please tell me how you came to murdering anyone and why."

Mrs. Fontaine's face crumpled slightly. "It doesn't matter, does it? The only thing that matters is that I confess that I'm guilty."

Nancy moved closer to Mrs. Fontaine's chair and knelt beside her. "Excuse me, but we have reason to believe the deaths are connected to the mysterious Templar horseman. That could not have possibly been you."

Mrs. Fontaine's expression changed again. This time, Alexandra saw fear.

"Of course I am no horseman. That was only some poor soul looking for the treasure that's buried under the temple." Her mood abruptly changed now from fear to nervous agitation. "It's really there, you know. Part of the Templar's treasure. No one knows how much, but. . . . More than one man has come here wanting to take it. Perhaps this one was a bit overly dramatic. I suggest you ignore the whole thing."

"Mrs. Fontaine," Nicholas said, his voice quiet, "I'm truly sorry to do this, but I must go for Constable Snow and bring him back here. He will arrest you, of course."

"Of course," Mrs. Fontaine said. "I'm ready."

"Don't go yet," Alexandra said. "Mrs. Fontaine needs to answer one more question." She turned toward her. "Why are you protecting the killer?"

"Protecting? I don't understand."

"You didn't kill anyone," Alexandra said, "but you know who did."

"My dear, I have no need to protect anyone, and I just told you, I am the guilty one." She was still stroking a cat in her lap who had fallen asleep and was snoring loudly.

"You are not the killer, but you should tell us who is," Alexandra said.

"What are you saying?" said a flabbergasted Nicholas. "Who is she taking the blame for?"

"It's someone she's known for a long time," Alexandra answered. "Though I don't understand why this person would allow Mrs. Fontaine to take the blame. It seems a cruel and heartless thing to do to someone who has been so kind to everyone in the village, but then, of course, we must accept that anyone capable of murder is capable of anything."

"Stop trying to blame someone else." Mrs. Fontaine's voice was choked. "I killed those people."

"Very well," Alexandra said, "if that's the case, tell me why."

Mrs. Fontaine looked up at Alexandra, confusion mixed with her tears. "Why? They were all bad men."

"You don't really believe that," Alexandra said. "You've had good things to say about almost all of them in the past."

Mrs. Fontaine took a shuddering breath. "There are things I know about all of them that no one else knows." Her expression was something akin to pleading. She wanted to be believed.

Alexandra studied her face for a moment. "All right, my lord" she said, turning to Nicholas. "Bring the constable here. And bring Judith Payne as well. She will want to know who killed her father."

"Don't bring her here!" Mrs. Fontaine's voice trembled. "Leave her alone. She's suffered enough."

Nicholas hesitated for a moment before a hint of understanding came into his eyes, and he moved toward the door,

In the meantime, Nancy picked up the cat sleeping in the chair next to Mrs. Fontaine's chair, and sat down. Holding the silver, silky creature in her lap, she leaned toward Mrs. Fontaine. "I must ask you a question unrelated to all of this." She spoke in a quiet voice as if she wanted the conversation to be confidential.

"What is it, Nancy?" Mrs. Fontaine, said, sounding terribly weary.

"It's about Dr. Gladstone's dog."

A surprised frown creased the elderly woman's forehead. "Zack?"

"Yes," Nancy said quietly and with a sly glance toward Alexandra, "He ate something poisonous, and I suspect it may be a plant growing in the doctor's garden. The doctor is no help," Nancy said, whispering. "She knows nothing about plants."

"What does this plant in her garden look like?" Mrs. Fontaine asked.

"Shrub-like, and the leaves are about like this," Nancy said, holding her thumb and forefinger about an inch apart, "and the flowers are purplish with yellow spots. Lots of seeds.

The plants spread themselves everywhere. I thought 'twas a weed at first, but perhaps not. Not much scent to the flowers."

"Rhododendron, I should say, and yes, it is indeed poisonous to animals," Mrs. Fontaine said. "Dogs as well as cats. That's why I never grow it. You must caution Dr. Gladstone to have them removed."

"I'll do my best," Nancy whispered.

Alexandra, who had been feigning disinterest, glanced involuntarily at Nancy, surprised that she had lied so easily. Nancy knew there were few flowers at all and no rhododendron growing in her garden. Obviously, Nancy suspected, just as she did, that the popular flower as the source of the poison for all the victims, including Zack. She wanted to find out whether or not Mrs. Fontaine cultivated them in her garden.

"I hope you gave poor Zack something to help him expel the poison," Mrs. Fontaine added.

"Oh, I did," Nancy assured her. "I believe he will be all right, but I just wasn't certain what had caused it. Neither was the doctor. She knows about people, now doesn't she? But animals? I'm afraid not."

Mrs. Fontaine said nothing as Nancy kept her seat beside her. Alexandra, still sitting across the room, abandoned her pretense of sorting through her medical bag and moved to another chair nearer the two of them.

"You have known me all of my life," she said to Mrs. Fontaine, "and you've known my family all of your life."

Mrs. Fontaine nodded but with a distracted expression.

"I'm sure, then, that you can understand that I don't want you implicated in this sordid business."

Mrs. Fontaine took a deep breath and let it out slowly. "You are kind, my dear, but you must do your duty."

There was another silent, awkward stretch of time until Nicholas finally returned with Constable Snow and Judith Payne in tow.

Judith rushed toward Mrs.Fontaine as soon as she entered and knelt beside her. "Oh, my dear lady, please tell me, what is this all about?"

Mrs. Fontaine looked at her, agitated. "I told them to leave you out of this. It's no concern of yours. You must leave immediately."

Judith was equally surprised. "But. . . . I don't understand. I was told—Constable Snow, Lord Dunsford--they said you asked for me, that you were distressed about something. They wouldn't tell me why."

"They lied to you," Mrs. Fontaine said. "Now you must leave."

"Mrs. Fontaine has just admitted that she committed all the recent murders of Freemasons here in Newton-upon-Sea, as well as that of your own father," Alexandra said.

Judith jumped to her feet. The blood drained from her face, leaving it a sickly pale, and her eyes were wide and fear-filled.

"Alexandra! Shush!" Mrs. Fontaine scolded. Agitated, she tried to rise from her chair. "Judith, leave immediately."

"I don't understand." Judith's voice was weak and trembling.

By contrast, Alexandra's voice was firm. "You don't understand that Mrs. Fontaine has just confessed to the murders you yourself committed?"

Judith's face had turned a sickly color. "I've killed no one."

"You're willing to allow Mrs. Fontaine to take the blame and pay for the crimes with her life?" Alexandra asked.

"I. . . ."

"Stop it!" Mrs. Fontaine said. "Stop trying to make her confess. I'm the guilty one."

There was a moment or chilling silence until Constable Snow finally spoke. "Very well, Mrs. Fontaine, stand please, and place your hands behind your back."

As Mrs. Fontaine struggled to get to her feet, Judith took a step toward Snow. "You're going to put her in manacles?"

Snow didn't answer, but the manacles made a clanking sound as he pulled them from a strap attached to his trousers. He helped Mrs. Fontaine up and clasped one side of the metal restraints on one of her wrists.

"Wait!" Judith cried. "Take those monstrous things off of her."

"It is my duty, Miss Payne, however unpleasant it may be," Snow said without looking at her. He secured Mrs. Fontaine's other wrist with both hands behind her back. The old woman was slightly stooped, as if the was uncomfortable, and waited to be led away. When Snow took her arm to guide her, she made her way toward the door in slow but unfaltering steps.

"You can't do that! She is innocent!" Judith cried. She turned toward Alexandra and spoke in an angry voice. "You're right, Dr. Gladstone, I killed them. All of them. Yes, my father as well. He deserved it more than any of them."

"Judith, I am old," Mrs. Fontaine said. "My life is almost over. You are young with everything to live for."

Still holding Mrs. Fontaine's arm, Snow turned to Judith. "What do you mean, your father deserved it more than any of them?"

Dropping into one of the chairs, she covered her face with her hands. When she looked up, she had regained some of her color, and she looked directly at the constable. "You would have been next, Constable," she said. "You're just like the others—no better."

Snow did not respond.

"You were lying about your father killing your suitors," Alexandra said. "Why?"

"My father tried to kill my own spirit by dictating who I could marry, by forbidding me to marry the man I loved. Isn't that worse than anything I've done? To try to destroy a person's spirit? To assume you have that right just because you are male? But worse, he wouldn't allow me to go to school. I am a mere seamstress, when I could have been more!"

Snow took a key from his pocket and unlocked the manacles while Mrs. Fontaine shook with sobs and repeated, "No, Judith, no, no."

Nancy went to her side and led her upstairs. When Judith tried to follow, Alexandra and Constable Snow stopped her, each with a hand on one of her arms.

"Why did those men—or Constable Snow--deserve to die?" Alexandra asked. "And what gave you the right to decide?"

"I did it because no one else would. I did it for justice. For the rights of women!" Judith shouted. Agitation had changed her face from white to red.

"Justice?" asked a baffled Alexandra. "The rights of women? I don't understand," Alexandra said.

Judith gave her a look of disdain. "I admired you so much, but I see now that you have become complacent like most women."

"Perhaps you could explain," Nicholas said. "All those men you poisoned were decent, upstanding men."

"Poisoned?" Judith asked. "How could you possibly know that?"

"Dr. Gladstone," Nicholas nodded at Alexandra, " is the one who realized you'd poisoned them with honey made by bees who'd eaten the pollen of your rhododendrons. Although I didn't know you kept bee,s as Mrs. Fontaine did."

"I discovered them once when I was trying to keep Zack from destroying her garden, but I didn't put it all together at first," Alexandra said.

"Clever," Nicholas said before he turned to Judith. "You may think her complacent, but she is a remarkably intelligent woman and an astute doctor."

"Yes, intelligent and astute," Judith said, her voice full of rage. "Those qualities matter not to the world, though, because she is woman. Her gender holds her back, just as it does me. Am I less decent and upstanding than those men who held me back?"

"Held you back?" Nicholas said. "How did all those men you killed hold you back?"

"They denied me the right to Freemasonry!" she shrieked.

"My dear, Miss Payne, you are quite irrational," Snow said. "You, as well as the rest of the world know that Freemasonry is a brotherhood."

"Ha! What of your Masonic devotion to equality? Are women excluded from equality? Is it not a good thing for womanhood to aspire to the betterment of all people? To benevolence and devotion to God? To freedom of the individual mind, to the great attributes of a World Order? When you deny a woman admission to your ranks, you are denying yourself, and you have become a hypocrite! Your aprons that symbolize purity are hypocritical. It made me sick to think about it when I sewed each one for all those men. Symbol of purity, you say! I smeared each one with blood from my own body. I defiled them the way you have defiled words like *equality* and *freedom*!"

"Miss Payne, surely you know that your own father—"

"The worst of a bad lot" she said, interrupting Snow. "The descendent of a founding member of the Temple of the Ninth Daughter who denied his own daughter the opportunity to make the world a better place by joining your numbers. Oh, how I admired my father's devotion to making the world a better place through Freemasonry. The same devotion was present in his father, and his grandfather, and all of the Payne men before him. It is my calling, my destiny, to be among those who stand for such beauty, but without your hypocrisy."

Snow's voice was remarkable in its calmness. "Freemasons cannot be all painted with the brush of hypocrisy, and certainly not the Lodge of the Ninth Daughter."

"Ah yes, the ninth daughter," she said. "That name is itself ludicrous. You christen yourselves in the memory of a woman, the ninth daughter. The ninth of the nine muses. She was Calliope, the goddess of inspiration, the muse for Homer's works. You name yourselves for a goddess and forbid women to join your ranks."

"None of what you say justifies murder," Nicholas said.

"Leave her alone!" Mrs. Fontaine said. "She's a distraught child." The woman's sudden appearance in the doorway surprised everyone in the room. Nancy stood behind her, looking worried.

"I'm sorry," Nancy said. "I tried to keep her calm and away from all of this."

"It's all right, Nancy," Alexandra said.

At the same time, Snow spoke. "She is no child, Mrs. Fontaine. However, I don't doubt that she is distraught, since she just confessed to murder." He turned back to Judith. "And I also believe that you are the person who chased Dr. Gladstone and Nancy as well. Dressed as a man."

"Yes, I dressed as a Templar and a man, disguising myself as my own enemy. Amusing! But empowering—such freedom not to be encumbered by skirts! And yes, I went after Dr. Gladstone and Nancy both. I had to. They stood in my way. I had to frighten the doctor, and I had to drug Nancy, but I wouldn't kill them. They are women. They are the ones I fight for."

"The ones you killed for," Snow said.

Mrs. Fontaine grew more agitated at Snow's words. "The poor girl has just lost her father. She—"

"She killed her father," Alexandra said, "and you insist on trying to protect her. "Why?"

"Because of her family! The Paynes are one of the old line families, just like my husband's, the Fontaines. They are French names—Paen and Fontaine. My maiden name was Payne, spelled differently when the family was in France long ago. They and others are fathers of the Templars." Mrs. Fontaine's voice grew more agitated. "Our French ancestors established the Temple of the Ninth Daughter on sacred ground that once belonged to the Templars, and where they buried part of their treasure. Don't forget the Templars wanted to change all of Europe and move it away from the tyranny of rogue churchmen and the tyranny of feudalism."

"Mrs. Fontaine, please. . ." Snow began.

"She taught me so much," Judith said. "She made me determined to carry out their ideals." Judith laughed, a cruel sound. "I only wish I'd known about that treasure legend. I could have used that to deflect all of you."

Mrs. Fontaine shook her head. "I wanted you to understand," she said, speaking to Judith. "I never meant for you to. . . You never knew how much I loved you. Your father, my kinsman, he did all he could for you. Especially after your mother died. You had to live your life without her love. I wanted to give you all the love I had. I don't understand what happened. The murders, posing as a Templar and terrorizing the village. I never meant for you to lose your senses and. . ."

"Don't condemn me!" Judith cried. "Can't you see? I did it for you as much as for me. I did it for all of womankind. For the ideal of equality. That's one of the Freemason's tenets, isn't it? One of the ideals that fired the Reformation. That was because of Freemasonry, but then a noble group became hypocrites who forgot their mission."

"Freemasonry is a system of morality," Snow said. He had already taken out his manacles again, and he soon had them attached to Judith's wrists.

"I am at peace with my own morals," she cried as he led her toward the door. "It is the deepest morality when one fights for one's own rights."

Mrs. Fontaine stood at her door and watched Judith and the constable until they disappeared from sight. "A tragedy," she said in a voice that was almost a whisper. "Such a tragedy to see one of the old-line descendants fall so far."

"It is a tragedy when anyone becomes so delusional," Alexandra said. "It matters not from what family they descend."

"Another tragedy is that some of this might have been curtailed if Constable Snow hadn't been so derelict in his duties," Nancy said.

Mrs. Fontaine's eyes flamed as she turned toward Nancy. "Don't dare blame poor Robert for any of this!"

Nancy was taken aback at her sudden show of anger. "I only meant to say that because he disappeared for his own selfish personal reasons--"

"You have no idea, Nancy," Mrs. Fontaine said with another show of anger. "His reasons are far from selfish. Each time he has been called away to London it's because of his sister. The poor woman has. . . ." Mrs. Fontaine's voice trailed off, and she turned away, covering her face with her hands. "Oh no, I didn't mean to say that. He wouldn't . . . ."

"I never knew Constable Snow had a sister in London," Nancy said.

"He never wanted people to know that she. . . ." Mrs. Fontaine paused again, tears filling her eyes.

"You don't have to say anything more," Alexandra said.

"No, you must know the truth. It's not right for people to malign him. He goes to London to help his sister, an invalid who had a child out of wedlock. Some man took advantage of the poor girl when she was no more than Charlotte Malcolm's age. Robert sees after her and her son. The boy must be at least seven years old now, and in need of educating. Robert. . . . Well, you mustn't blame him when he's called away. He only wants to protect both of them."

"I'm sorry," Nancy said. "I didn't know. . . ."

Mrs. Fontaine, looking weary, sat down in her chair and was immediately joined by three of her cats. "There is much people don't know about their own neighbors in this village," she said. "Newton-upon-Sea is full of secrets."

Epilogue

Zack stood at a distance from Nicholas as he sat, sipping brandy in Alexandra's parlor. The big dog's eyes followed his every move, but without his usual cautionary stance.

"At least he's not snarling," Nicholas said to Alexandra, in a chair next to him, the sling crutch propped on the arm of the chair. Nancy was a few feet away, arranging plates on a cart.

"He's beginning to trust you, at least a little." Alexandra motioned for Zack to lie down. The dog obeyed but still without redirecting his eyes.

"Speaking of trust, it was obviously wrong for us not to trust Constable Snow," Nicholas said. "You were right about one thing, Nancy, old girl," Nicholas said. "It really *was* a woman that drew the constable away. As a matter of fact, I finally received a telegram from Captain Mitchell at Scotland Yard confirming that he regularly sees after his sister."

Nancy's eyes widened. "What else did the captain say?"

Nicholas set his glass aside and glanced at Alexandra and then at Nancy. "Mrs. Fontaine was right about his visiting London often to see about his sister and her son, but this time it seems his visit was more urgent than usual. The child was about to be taken away to gaol for stealing money from a woman who employed him at a dame school."

"I've heard of those schools," Nancy said. "People put children to work in exchange for teaching them to read, and usually the teacher can hardly read herself."

Nicholas nodded. "Seems he had a job weaving straw for hats. Snow convinced the police the boy took money to buy food for his mother."

"And that saved the child?" Alexandra shook her head. "Usually an innocent motive makes no difference."

"Apparently Snow was quite persuasive. Either that or someone owed him a favor. I've offered to pay for the boy's education at a public school."

Nancy shook her head. "Never would have guessed the truth."

"Just one of the many secrets of Newton-upon-Sea Mrs. Fontaine mentioned," Nicholas said. "How do you suppose she knows so much?"

"She's lived here all of her life, and that's quite a long time," Alexandra said.

Nicholas took a sip of his brandy. "Quite so, but that doesn't explain how she knew Judith was a killer."

"There's more to Mrs. Fontaine than longevity," Alexandra said. "She's remarkably intelligent. She put all the clues together just as we did."

"Intelligent, indeed," Nicholas said, "and fiercely protective of those she cares about—Constable Snow as well as Judith. Like you, Nancy, I never would have guessed the old boy's true reason for being away, but I must say, contrary to what you originally believed, it was hard for me to imagine him with a woman."

"I should say it would have been equally as hard to imagine Judith murdering anyone," Alexandra added.

"Mmm," Nicholas said, nodding. "Not to mention poisoning Zack. Who would have thought she could do that?"

"She didn't poison him," Alexandra said. "He did that to himself."

"Oh come now, you know as well as I that Nancy made up that preposterous story about his eating rhododendrons in your garden just to get Mrs. Fontaine talking."

"That was clever of you," Alexandra said, turning to Nancy

"Thank you, Miss Alex," Nancy said with a smile. "Zack's poisoning came from tulip bulbs," she added. "He dug them up in Mrs. Fontaine's garden on his own."

"And how did you determine that?" Nicholas asked.

"Miss Alex told me," Nancy said.

"I saw him digging in her garden." Alexandra said. "I was embarrassed, of course, but it never occurred to me at first what exactly he'd dug up. Not until I remembered that was the area she always had tulips growing."

"Fortunate they didn't kill him," Nicholas said.

"They're not as lethal to pets as, say, rhododendrons," Alexandra said. "I found that interesting fact in one of my father's books. Reading that text and digging into the pathology of poison in dogs is what got me thinking about poison in all those human victims, so I did even more research in those medical texts, just as I told you. And you're right, I am fortunate. What would I have done if Zack had not been well enough to help rescue me when I was in the ravine?"

"Yes, you're as lucky as Zack. And so is Nancy," he added. "If Judith poisoned you, Nancy, as she did all those men, you're incredibly lucky you didn't die as they did."

"Judith never meant for Nancy or me to die," Alexandra said. "She wanted to frighten us, yes, but I have concluded that Nancy was merely given a rather strong dose of codeine. Not enough to be lethal, but enough to leave her addled for a while. Nancy and I came to that conclusion by discussing her symptoms."

"Remarkable women, you two."

"You're too kind," Alexandra said, trying not be embarrassed. "And speaking of remarkable, I must say, you deserve that accolade as much as anyone. It is truly wonderful how you and the boys persevered in trying to find me as well as how you rescued me. How can I ever thank you?"

"Well my dear," Nicholas said, "speaking for myself, I can only say you've already given me a most remarkable and cherished thank-you when you were in Dr. Abercrombie's surgery."

"I'm afraid I don't remember," Alexandra said.

"Oh, but you must remember. You called me darling."

Alexandra felt her face grow warm. "I called you. . . ? Surely I didn't say—"

"Your exact words were, *Yes, my darling. I'm going to be quite all right.*"

Alexandra blushed even deeper and stammered a few incomprehensible words before she final managed to ask the question she detested when it was asked of her.

"Are you quite sure?"

At the same time, Zack raised himself from his favorite position in front of the hearth and took a step toward Nicholas, a menacing growl rumbling from his throat.

CPSIA information can be obtained
at www.ICGtesting.com
Printed in the USA
FSHW010505240221
78902FS